SPACERS

WARTORN 3 CLUSTER

MIRTH PUBLISHING
ST. JOHN'S

SCOTT BARTLETT

WARTORN CLUSTER

© Scott Bartlett 2020

Cover art by: Tom Edwards (tomedwardsdesign.com)

Typography and interior formatting by: Steve Beaulieu (facebook.com/BeaulisticBookServices)

Library and Archives Canada Cataloguing in Publication

Bartlett, Scott

Wartorn Cluster / Scott Bartlett ; illustrations by Tom Edwards ; typography and interior formatting by Steve Beaulieu.

ISBN 978-1-988380-22-3

To Eldon Adams. I would be nowhere without my readers. Thank you, Eldon, for your incredible support of my writing.

CHAPTER 1

New Houston, Oasis Colony
Gabbro System, The Brush
Earth Year 2290

Captain Simon Moll turned toward his Tactical officer, though he found himself hesitating before giving his order.

The pause drew a glance from his XO, Commander Lane, and Moll cleared his throat. "I want updated targeting data on all eight Red Sky ships positioned around the Rodney Percival Station."

"Targeting data, sir?" The tactical officer's eyebrows twitched upward.

"You heard me. Ops, relay the same orders to the other destroyers. I want everyone ready to fire on a moment's notice."

"Aye, sir."

Why did I hesitate? He'd given the order to target those ships a thousand times before, and there was a chance he'd have to do it again, perhaps many more times. He knew exactly how this confrontation with the Russian corp, Red Sky, was going to play out.

Barely anything caused him to hesitate anymore. Why did this?

I'm less certain of myself, this time around. There is a new factor at play.

Unbidden, the name crossed his mind: *Tad Thatcher.*

The man Moll both needed and feared, just as he feared the addition of any new element. Reality was a delicate balance of factors—a balance Moll had been tinkering with for an impossibly long time. Every new addition brought the risk of toppling everything, and crushing him in the process, along with any hope of ever achieving his goal.

Barta Adami, his Ops officer, spoke up from her station. "Sir, the Red Sky ships are forming up in defensive formation around Rodney Percival. I also have a transmission from Captain Redding of the *Archimedes*, who wishes to speak with you."

"Put him through."

Redding appeared in the holotank at the fore of the CIC. "Sir, I have to question why you've asked us to compile targeting data. Red Sky has always treated us well. Surely you don't mean to fire on them?"

Moll closed his eyes, reaching for his next line, which he'd delivered so many times before. Redding was a troublemaker, just like Red Sky's CEO, Mikhail Volkov. But at least he wouldn't have to put up with Redding for much longer. "I *do* mean to fire on them, Captain Redding. However, I can assure you that we will leave all of their ships intact."

Redding blinked. "Then you mean to fire on them as an intimidation tactic?"

"That's correct."

"That will still irreparably damage our relations with Red Sky."

Moll chuckled. "Boris, soon Sunder Incorporated will be so powerful that it will make no difference what opinion a gadfly like Red Sky has of us."

The man's complexion whitened at that. "Very well, Captain. Thank you for taking the time to explain that to me."

"Dismissed." Moll nodded curtly at Adami, who terminated the connection.

Forty-one minutes later, the six Sunder destroyers entered real-time comms range with the Red Sky ships, who had all raised shields. The battle group protecting Rodney Percival Station, which held the Russian corp's HQ, consisted of a destroyer, three corvettes, two cruisers, a frigate, and a logistics ship.

"Get me Volkov," Moll told Adami.

"Aye, sir."

Actually putting him in touch with the Red Sky CEO took some doing, as it turned out he wasn't aboard the *Burnyi*, the destroyer he captained, but seeing to some business aboard the station.

Mikhail Volkov appeared in the holotank wearing a scowl.

"I trust you know why I'm here, Mikhail?"

"Of course. You're here to demand passage through Gabbro System. But my position hasn't changed, Moll. I see what you are doing in The Brush. What you call an aggressive marketing campaign, I call coercion. This isn't just a protection racket. You're conquering this region."

True mirth filled Moll's chest at that, and it escaped as hearty laughter.

Volkov's face reddened. "You dare mock me?"

"I dare a lot more than that, Mikhail. Your misapprehension of the situation is so perfect and complete that I find it extremely funny." Moll wiped a tear from his eye. "I have to thank you for that."

"I've misapprehended nothing."

"Oh, but you have. For one, you seem to be under the impression that your assessment of Sunder's behavior is of any consequence. It isn't. But most comedic of all is that you think

I'm here to *demand* anything. Mikhail, I am here merely to blow your ships from space unless you pick up and leave Gabbro, immediately."

Volkov's eyes widened. "Leave Gabbro? We're headquartered here."

"Not anymore. Take what you can carry and leave, Mikhail. I offer you this opportunity as a courtesy. I'll only offer it once."

"You can't force us out of our home system, Moll."

"Who's going to stop me? The UNC? You know as well as I do that they don't enforce anything, anymore." Without bothering to severe the connection with Volkov, Moll turned to his Ops officer. "Have all ships fire primary lasers on that frigate."

"Aye, sir." Adami tapped at her console with her usual efficiency.

Volkov's face had paled, reminding Moll of his conversation with Boris Redding. "You have to be bluffing. Surely Sunder has not sunk so low."

"I wish I were bluffing, Mikhail. I wish your stubbornness hadn't brought us to this."

Bright beams lanced across the tactical display shown on Moll's screen. The other Red Sky ships failed to react as the frigate's forcefield shuddered violently, then fell. *They know we had them beat the moment we entered the system with six destroyers.*

"Stop," Volkov spat. "Stop! We'll leave Gabbro."

"Have our ships cease fire, Adami."

The laserfire ceased. The frigate's hull was scorched, but only superficial damage had been done.

Moll turned a smile toward the Red Sky CEO. "You have twenty-four hours, Mikhail. Show me any sign of hesitation, and weapons fire will resume."

With that, he motioned for Adami to terminate the connection.

CHAPTER 2

New Houston, Oasis Colony
Freedom System, Dupliss Region
Earth Year 2290

THE MARQUEE ABOVE THE STAGE FLASHED, THEN DISPLAYED ITS new scrolling message:

"VERONICA ROSE, SINGING 'I'VE GOT YOU UNDER MY SKIN.'"

Thatcher's eyes met the Frontier CEO's across the tabletop at the back of the bar. "You put your name in?" What he really meant was, *You can sing?*

She winked at him, then bounded up from her seat, taking her cocktail with her. Her usual veneer of professionalism had vanished, and while she was still just as composed, the fact she was on her fourth drink of the night wasn't doing much for Thatcher's own composure.

Her gait was steady as she crossed the bar—it involved more swaying, but it was steady. He cleared his throat as he averted his eyes, forcing himself to stare at the stage.

If she gets sloppy tonight, it will be Frontier that suffers.

Which means all of Dupliss will suffer, if not the entire Dawn Cluster.

Could that really be true? Could an entire star cluster's fate really be impacted by a single night of indiscretion?

Probably not. But the balance of power throughout the Cluster had gotten so uncertain that it seemed anything might topple it. And like it or not, Frontier *was* a corp that others had started to look to, hoping to see signals for how they should act.

I'm worrying, he realized. But he came by that habit honestly. Thatchers had been worrying since well before humanity had hauled itself out of Earth's gravity well—since before the song Rose was about to sing had been written. Thatcher knew the song was from one of Earth's most famous crooners, but he couldn't place his name.

What am I doing here? He found himself taking a long sip from his neat whiskey as he contemplated the question. It wasn't only his immediate environment that prompted the thought—a karaoke bar filled with drunken civilians and slightly more sober Frontier employees—protected and protectors, mingling freely.

He also wondered how he'd come to work for a corp that was about to go up against an alliance twenty times its size. How did stabilizing the Dawn Cluster in order to fight the Xanthic fit into *that?*

Thatcher knew how, of course. If they allowed the Daybreak Combine to continue gobbling up the Cluster, then they would have stability, all right. Stability for pirates. Free rein for them to pillage this side of the galaxy, and then maybe Earth Local Space, if the wormhole ever reopened.

If it came to that, the United Nations and Colonies would probably give the Combine a run for their money, but it might be a near thing. Especially if Daybreak was given years to exploit the entire Cluster's resources. To solidify their rule.

No, Daybreak had to fall, along with its leader, Herwin Dirk. Still…it felt like a frustrating distraction from the mission he'd been sent here to complete: unite the Cluster. Stabilize. And prepare humanity to fight the Xanthic.

Rose was adjusting the mic atop the stand that extended from the stage. She'd all but ordered him to come along tonight, insisting it would be good for the citizens of New Houston to see Frontier executives and military personnel as normal people—accessible and open.

Thatcher crossed his arms. Plenty of people had gawked at him since he'd entered the bar, but none had approached him, and he certainly hadn't accosted them. He'd never been good at schmoozing. He saw protecting people like the ones at this bar as the foundation of everything he did, but that didn't mean he should have to make small talk with anyone.

Nothing Frontier does is small. Why diminish that?

Thatcher's eyes fell on Mittelman, who sat with his back against the plush couch that ran along the entirety of the bar's back wall. The man was fiddling with his eyepiece, and when he finished whatever he was doing, he sat still, his head leveled at the stage. Unmoving.

"You're recording her," Thatcher said. It wasn't a question.

"Of course."

"Without her permission?"

The spymaster's eyes met Thatcher's, though he didn't turn his head—else his eyepiece would follow, diminishing the recording. "Do you really think half the people in here aren't recording her already? It's *Veronica Rose,* CEO of Frontier Security. We're the reason this colony hasn't been obliterated, or enslaved. Of course they want to remember this night." Mittelman shrugged slightly. "Besides, she'll be disappointed if I *don't* record her. The vid will look great to civilians and employees both, when it starts making the rounds on the system intranet."

"Everything's PR," Thatcher muttered. The music had already begun, and now Rose began singing. Thatcher and

Mittelman could still talk as he recorded—Thatcher had no doubt the eyepiece's software was sophisticated enough to filter out their voices.

"Of course everything's PR," Mittelman said. "Veronica Rose is one of the most calculated people I know. And she's good at it…for one reason. Well, for a lot of reasons, but without this one thing nothing would work."

"What is it?" Thatcher asked, knowing Mittelman would wait until the question was asked and wanting to get it over with.

"She believes in what she does. Really, truly believes. Propaganda gets a bad rep, you know. It has to come from a place of honesty, or it doesn't work. You have to really believe in what you're putting out there. If Rose herself didn't believe in establishing free space, no one else would. But she does believe in it. So it's catching fire all across the Cluster."

Thatcher nodded. It made sense. And since he worked for Frontier, then officially, he believed in free space too. But he did wonder how viable it really was. Letting anyone ship goods through the systems you controlled. Granting mining rights freely to the highest bidder, regardless of their affiliation. In theory, it sounded ideal. In practice, it seemed like a good way to let your enemies slip past your defenses.

But Rose believed in it vehemently, and Mittelman was right that the idea was resonating with people all over the Cluster. If free space brought people to Frontier's cause—and more importantly, if it brought reinforcements to their cause—then Thatcher wouldn't oppose it. They would need all the help they could get in the coming war.

Besides, if he started speaking against free space, then Rose was liable to lump him in with the likes of Ramon Pegg and Herwin Dirk. He'd definitely be out of a job, then…and no matter how he felt about Rose's utopian ideals, he would never go to work for scum like Pegg and Dirk.

Mittelman spoke again. "So, when are you going to bed with her?"

Thatcher stiffened, his eyes snapping up from the tabletop, where he'd been gazing as he lost himself in thought. "With who?" he said, his voice quiet but steely.

"You know who I mean. Rose."

"You're out of line."

Mittelman smirked, though his head remained leveled at the stage. "You'll drop your Earther morality sooner or later, Commander. No one in the Cluster can afford to hold onto luxuries like that for long."

"I have a wife waiting for me on Earth. A *pregnant* wife."

"Waiting on the moon, you mean. You know as well as I do that Earth was taken by the Xanthic."

"They appeared there, and civilians were evacuated, yes. But I'm sure it's been retaken by now. And when the wormhole reopens—"

"But that's just it. The wormhole *isn't* going to reopen, because there is no wormhole left to open. Every last trace of it has dissipated into the void."

Thatcher's jaw had begun to ache, and he forced himself to stop clenching it. In his mind's eye, he saw the Xanthic swarming through the temporary wormhole the aliens had created over Recept. They'd escaped his fleet, and gone who knew where. "I'm *going* to return to her."

"How?"

"I'll find a way."

The spymaster shrugged once more. Then he removed his eyepiece, folded it, and slipped it into an inside pocket of his unstructured navy blazer. Thatcher realized the song was over, and he cast his eyes across the room—there was Rose, ordering yet another drink.

"You'll move on with your life eventually, I'm sure." Mittelman's voice carried undertones of smug amusement. Which wasn't much different from any other time. "Sooner or later, every widower does."

Thatcher turned back toward the man, and he felt glad his hands were under the table as they curled into fists.

He's trying to bait me. Why? Is he testing me, like I've seen him test others? Or has he decided I'm a threat and wants to take me down?

Thoughts of throttling the spymaster flitted through his head, his mind churning out a surprising variety of murder fantasies in record time.

But it would take more than a spider like Mittelman to ruffle his calm. During battle, Thatcher regularly faced his own mortality and kept his cool. At least a couple of times, death had seemed certain. Yet here he was. All because he'd kept control of himself.

He would keep control now.

"What did I miss?" Rose said, her voice bright and bubbly as she returned holding three drinks.

Her face fell as she took in Thatcher's expression.

He rose from the table. "I was just leaving."

CHAPTER 3

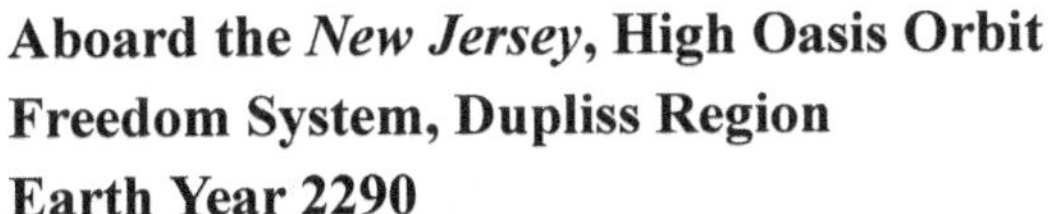

Aboard the *New Jersey*, High Oasis Orbit
Freedom System, Dupliss Region
Earth Year 2290

"IT BECOMES A TIGHTER FIT FROM HERE, CAPTAIN." THE NARROW passage between the *New Jersey*'s inner and outer hulls forced them to sidle, and Thatcher's XO was having trouble turning his head to address his captain. "Since we reshuffled the modules, I've been fielding no end of complaints from the lower ranks in Engineering. They're the ones who get sent into places like these, more often than not."

Candle was babbling, Thatcher noted. Between that and his constant warnings that the maintenance corridors would be cramped, it was getting a little annoying.

He forced himself to take a deep breath—as deeply as he could, inside these confines. "That was good work, shifting the port primary capacitor module back against those attitude jets." Thatcher had occupied positions of authority for long enough to know when a subordinate was fishing for compliments, and this was definitely one of those times.

"Thank you, sir."

Thatcher nodded, which Candle couldn't see, and the motion scraped his ear against a valve jutting out from his right. *Damn it,* he thought, though he gave no audible indication of the event. He'd long ago learned to do his cursing *inside* his head.

Complimenting his crew was something he knew he needed to do more of. That was almost as important as learning to trust them more. At least, according to Rose it was.

The Frontier CEO didn't dispense such advice lightly. In fact, it came pretty close to an order. Indeed, Thatcher had his suspicions that he'd been back-benched during his ship's repairs and upgrades so that he'd have plenty of time to reflect on her words. He hadn't asked if that was the case, and she'd offered neither a confirmation nor a denial of his suspicions.

But he couldn't help asking himself why he hadn't been given another ship while the *New Jersey* was dry-docked at Helio Base Five. More importantly: why hadn't he been placed in command of a bigger ship yet? A destroyer, maybe? He knew he hadn't been with Frontier all that long, but still…

"The reshuffling allowed us to take a more balanced approach," Thatcher said, the passageway growing more narrow with every step. "Moving that module back made room for more repair drones, not to mention the extra capacitor module, which makes me feel better about taking the *Jersey* on a long haul… about taking the fight to Daybreak. But even so. We're down a missile tube now, and I'm concerned our old girl is slowly being outclassed by the enemy. They keep growing in size and number, and the *Jersey* only has so much space for modules."

Candle nodded slowly. "That thought has crossed my mind a few times too, sir. But she's gotten us through some tight spots. I'm willing to bet she's not done teaching the Cluster how a real warship shows up to a fight." He came to a sudden halt, and Thatcher nearly collided with him, even inching along as they were. "Here's the weld you wanted to inspect."

Candle squeezed himself back against an atmosphere duct while Thatcher ran a hand along the weld, where the primary capacitor module met the new repair drone storage. The storage module wasn't a conventional size or shape—it had needed to be cut from an existing module to meet the light cruiser's unique needs. Under Thatcher's fingers, the welding was about as rough as it gets, bumpy and uneven. But it would hold.

He nodded to himself. Some captains wouldn't have been caught dead in crawlspaces like these, but he wouldn't have been able to sleep properly without having laid eyes on each new modification to his ship. He knew every inch of the *New Jersey*. He felt connected to her, deep down in his bones. He had to know she'd hold together when he needed her to.

If I'm good to her, she'll be good to me. Another of his grandfather's sayings, parading through his mind.

Thatcher gave the weld one last pat. "It'll do."

"Glad to hear it, sir."

He sniffed, then forced himself to smile, hoping it didn't look too ghastly in the dim, red-lit passage. In his mind's eye, Rose's face appeared, nodding at him encouragingly. "We've worked together long enough to drop the stiff formalities, don't you think? When we're away from the crew, at least. Like when we're squeezed inside the ship's outer hull, for instance." Thatcher pushed out a chuckle, to indicate his words had been a joke. "I'll call you Bill if you'll call me Tad."

"Tad, sir?"

Thatcher nodded.

"Okay, sir. Tad it is."

Thatcher tilted his head to one side, then shrugged. It was a start.

The *Jersey*'s old commander, Captain Vaughn, had called everyone by their first names in the CIC, Thatcher knew. He doubted he'd ever get there. But maybe this was a workable middle ground.

His comm buzzed from his hip holster, and he fished it out, raising it gingerly to avoid tearing his blue service uniform on an errant piece of metal. "Thatcher."

"Ensign Grey here, sir."

"You don't need to announce yourself every time you contact me, Ensign. I'll assume it's the Ops officer on duty unless I'm told otherwise."

"Yes, sir." Grey sounded embarrassed, as well he might—this was the third time Thatcher had corrected him for that. "Sorry, sir."

"Just try to remember going forward." Thatcher spoke as gently as he could, remembering the reason Grey been bumped up to primary Ops officer in the first place. "What was it you had to tell me?"

"Oh. The admiral just came aboard, sir. He's waiting in your office to meet you now."

Grey sounded more apprehensive with every word. For one, he'd called Captain Frederick Wilson by the wrong rank, but Thatcher could forgive that since everyone still called Wilson "the admiral." Besides, he doubted it was truly why Grey seemed nervous. That likely had more to do with his awareness that Thatcher was a stickler for protocol, and that he should have been notified of another captain's impending visit well before the man actually arrived on the ship.

He suppressed a sigh. Likely, Wilson had showed up on a random shuttle unannounced, without notifying anyone beforehand. He was that sort of man, Thatcher had learned: the sort who preferred to skip the pomp that came with command. Thatcher tended to think each arcane ritual had a reason, even when that reason wasn't immediately clear, and he didn't think they should be deviated from. But then, he respected Wilson enough that his more laid-back approach didn't diminish him any, in Thatcher's esteem.

"Tell the captain I'll be right there. I assume Chief Scott is already seeing to his comfort?"

"Aye, sir."

"Very good, Ensign." With that, Thatcher ended the call.

As he and Candle sidled back along the maintenance corridor, parting ways once they reached a regular passageway, Thatcher found himself missing his old primary Ops officer, Lieutenant Lucy Guerrero. She knew protocol like the back of her hand, and she'd had the sort of crisp efficiency Thatcher expected of himself. But he'd leaned on her too hard, and her disposition had proved more brittle than he'd originally assumed.

No. That's putting too much of the blame on her. Rose assigned a lot more of that responsibility to him, he knew, and that was how he needed to see it, too. It was why he was trying to change his approach to the crew, even though they respected him—even seemed to love him.

Some of them seemed to, anyway.

There was no time to change into another uniform, and on his way to the meeting, Thatcher frowned ferociously at the grease stains plaguing his arms, torso, and even his right pant leg. Wilson would be too polite to remark on it, he knew. Possibly, he wouldn't even notice. But it still bothered Thatcher.

"Tad." Wilson's smile could be heard in his voice as well as seen. He stood, opting for a handshake over a salute. Thatcher grasped the offered hand, unable to avoid catching the man's joviality even if he'd wanted to. "Always great to see you."

"The pleasure's mine, Fred. And the honor."

"Oh, come off it. Let's sit down and have a chat."

Two steaming mugs sat opposite each other on Thatcher's desk, sitting on granite coasters. He took an experimental sip upon sitting, and found the temperature exactly to his liking. Chief Scott had an uncanny knack for discerning Thatcher's preferences, even though he rarely communicated them to the man directly.

"I'm afraid we'll need to get right to business," Wilson said, setting his own mug down after a long sip. "With war on the horizon, now is not the time for small talk."

"Agreed. What brings you here, sir?"

Wilson shook his head. "None of that. We're the same rank now, so don't go sir-ing me."

Thatcher said nothing. They weren't the same rank in Space Fleet's eyes, and despite that the Fleet was a galaxy away, it still felt odd to think of Wilson as his equal.

"I've just received some intel from a mutual friend of ours—Hans Mittelman. He reports that Degenerate Empire is expanding into northern Dupliss."

Thatcher narrowed his eyes. "Unbelievable. How do they expect to hold onto anything with the forces they have?" It was true that the pirates had plenty of ships, but they were mostly underpowered. They also had five other regions to worry about, along with other hostile powers on Iberis' doorstep.

"They don't. Not with their own forces, anyway. They're using intimidation tactics to make vassals of the corps based in the systems they've taken."

Thatcher almost scoffed. *"Vassals?"*

Wilson nodded. "Things are getting positively medieval, north of here, Tad. Those corps were never particularly loyal to Frontier—indeed, a lot of them resent our getting the Oasis security contract over them. So I gather it was easy enough to coerce them."

"Those corps are full of cowards, then. They're not just going against us. They're also going against every civilian we're responsible for protecting."

"I agree with you. The next step is to convince *them* of that. Clearly, the so-called Empire is too weak to hold all the territories it's gobbled up. Now is the right time to hit them, while Daybreak is gathering their own forces. Hitting them starts with breaking up this vassal situation."

Thatcher's eyebrows rose and then settled again as he considered Wilson's words.

Help wasn't likely to come from the Dawn Cluster's south. While there were apparently plenty of corps down there positively disposed toward Frontier's cause, they were currently embroiled in conflicts of their own. It was just his luck that war had swept the south two weeks after Frontier had attacked Daybreak, sparking the conflict that would soon inflame the north.

"I'm with you," Thatcher said. "The *New Jersey* is with you. With Ms. Rose's blessing, of course."

"You already have it." Wilson smiled. "I'm glad to have you on board. I should go. We both have preparing to do."

Wilson rose from his seat and lifted a hand to the hatch's handle, but before he could leave, Thatcher spoke. "By the way. You mentioned Mittelman alerted you to this situation. What do you make of the man?"

When the former admiral turned from the hatch, his smile had become a wry grin. "He's exactly what you'd expect, isn't he?"

CHAPTER 4

New Houston, Oasis Colony
Freedom System, Dupliss Region
Earth Year 2290

It won't be very long, now, Mittelman thought.

He strode along the sun-dappled path with his hands clasped behind his back. Above him, tree branches shifted in the wind, doling out sunbeams randomly.

Moen Park was beautiful any time of year, but especially now, near spring's end, when the trees wore their full complement of leaves and the shade provided a pleasant counterpoint to the sun's warmth.

Its manicured paths all led to the hill at the park's center, and Mittelman headed there now, wondering as he went: how much longer would New Houston's residents be proud to have a park named after the founder of Sunder Incorporated? As much as any other Cluster dweller, Mittelman admired the pioneering spirit it had taken for Captain Patrick Moen to start one of the first private military corps in the Dawn Cluster. But he wondered how much longer the name "Sunder" would bear its shine for the people who lived here.

He made a bet with himself, then and there:

It won't be very long.

He reached the park's highest point, the hilltop where the shade ended. Here, the sun bathed him, its warmth just short of being uncomfortable. The hill offered a stunning view of New Houston, sprawled below, its sea of foliage shifting in the gentle breeze like a living thing.

Mittelman's favorite bench was occupied by the very man he'd come to Moen Park looking for. This man didn't know he was being sought by Mittelman, which made his sitting on the bench almost serendipitous. Mittelman didn't really believe in things like that, but he couldn't help thinking it all the same.

The man was in the dead center of the bench, which seemed somewhat inconsiderate. Mittelman sat on the end. "Enjoying your last day of planet leave?"

Lieutenant Commander William Candle—Billy, to most—turned to him, his expression of thoughtful blankness falling away to make room for one of mild amusement. "Harold Mills, isn't it? I don't officially know your real name." Candle chuckled. "Not officially."

Oh, how very clever.

"I *am* enjoying the day, to answer your question," Candle said when Mittelman didn't answer. "I'm not like the captain, who gets antsy every time his feet touch the ground. I'm the opposite. Spaceships make me antsy. After a while, anyway."

"The *New Jersey* would make me antsy too, if I had the weight that you bear on my shoulders."

Candle shrugged, his gaze returning to the shifting vista below. "Actually, it's the captain who shoulders most of the weight of command. He's just that kind of leader."

"I'm not talking about that weight. I'm talking about the stress that must accompany your...*other* task."

The XO's head cocked to one side as he turned back to Mittelman. "My other task?"

"Let me be more specific. I'm referring to the intelligence package you leave in a digital dead drop every time you visit Freedom System."

Candle froze, his stare fixed on Mittelman's face. The blood fled from his cheeks.

"That's what it is, isn't it?" Mittelman said. "An intelligence package? The only other use for a dead drop is to leak information to journalists, and I haven't seen any explosive revelations coming out of the *New Jersey*. Not any scandalous ones, anyway. Not yet."

Candle's silence stretched on.

"Relax. I haven't cracked the encryption, and I haven't figured out who the recipient is. Both are within my power, of course—it's just a matter of time. But I don't *have* to figure out either of them. I'm guessing it's worth a lot to you to keep both those things a secret. Which is why you're talking to me right now, and not getting fired by Veronica Rose."

"Does she know?"

"Of course not, you idiot. Any leverage I have over you would evaporate the moment I shared this with her."

"What do you want, then?"

Mittelman leaned back, putting both hands behind his head and drinking in the view. *Ah, New Houston.* He'd visited the original Houston once, and it looked nothing like this. Hot and sere—one of humanity's early experiments with large settlements in inhospitable environments. *Practice for living in space for long stretches at a time.* He wondered if the UNC would ever allow their species to evolve to the point where humans would live in space indefinitely.

"I'm still lacking a proper mole aboard the *Jersey*," Mittelman said at last. "And I haven't been able to crack the ship's systems, either, to place my scrapers. Thatcher has the benefit of Rose's best techs, unsurprisingly, and they give the cruiser's defenses a tune-up every time she enters orbit. But what better mole to have than Thatcher's own Executive Officer?"

Candle was looking out at New Houston again, his jaw rigid. "What sort of things do you want to know?"

"I'd like to know every time he shits. Let's start there."

CHAPTER 5

Aboard the *New Jersey*
Ramage System, Dupliss Region
Earth Year 2290

"Sir, Captain Wilson requests that we join Alpha Squadron in diverging from the ecliptic plane along the positive Z-axis."

Thatcher shifted in the captain's chair, wondering for the thousandth time since taking command of the *Jersey* what it would have cost to line each CIC chair with even thin cushioning. He would never request that, of course, but it would have been nice if the designers had considered the occupants' comfort just a little more than they had. "Acknowledged. Nav, make it happen. Grey, relay the order to the other Alpha vessels."

"Aye, sir."

It had taken the better part of a week to get Ensign Brian Grey to refer to Wilson by his proper rank, but Thatcher had finally achieved it. As for the order itself—well, it hadn't really been an order, had it? As Grey had said, Wilson had "requested" that the *Jersey* diverge from the ecliptic. He framed all his orders that way, at least the ones he sent to Thatcher. It was a nice gesture. An acknowledgment that not so long ago, Thatcher had been the one calling the shots for a Frontier fleet around this size. But he hoped Wilson didn't frame every order he gave as a request. The chain of command functioned the way it did for a reason.

"XO, make sure the missile crew on duty is prepped to load a second Hellborn the moment we fire the one already in the chamber." Thatcher certainly didn't frame any of his orders as requests.

"Aye, sir."

Grey twisted around in his seat, though he didn't quite meet his captain's eyes. He never did. *He's no Guerrero.* She at least had the balls to make eye contact, and to offer her view on things, even if it differed from Thatcher's. Only when it was appropriate to do so, of course. Mostly when it was appropriate.

"Sir, the Wellington force is adopting a defensive posture, with a fair spread—all across the ecliptic, though, with only minor deviations. Seems we should get a decent flank on them."

Thatcher felt his lip twitch at Grey's use of such inaccurate terms as "fair" and "decent." Yes, the holoscreen would give Thatcher precise figures, but no one wanted to squint at a readout in the middle of a pitched battle. Much better to make one's verbal reports precise in the first place. *I'll have to mention that to him.* There was just so much he needed to mention to Grey....

"Acknowledged," he said, keeping his annoyance out of his voice. They were here to make an example of Wellington Security Solutions, a corp that specialized in system defense, with a branch that focused exclusively on cybersecurity. Wellington was the main corporate muscle in Ramage System, but their relationship with their clients here—a wintry planet called Crystalline and a few belter habitats scattered around the system's periphery —had changed radically. Essentially, it was now a protection racket, with Wellington extorting heavy 'taxes' for the pirates who'd pressured them into becoming their vassals. A few other local corps had joined in on screwing civilians, all of them members of the Ramage Star Alliance: Skyworks, a space construction company; Corecorp, an asteroid mining outfit; and Pathways, an interstellar shipping company.

Not every corp had been willing to submit to Degenerate Empire. The Frontier force had encountered a flood of corporate-owned ships in the systems south of Ramage, all of them ousted from their home systems because they refused to play ball with pirates. It was the first time in Cluster history that corporations had been physically displaced from the systems they were based out of.

Veronica Rose was making hay from that specious sunshine. "Let it be known throughout the Cluster that Frontier Security stands against this evil practice," she'd said in her last broadcast. "Indeed, I hereby declare our home system, Freedom System, to be a free port, through which anyone is allowed to pass freely. We also welcome merchants and traders of all stripes. The only vessels to whom Freedom System is barred are those owned by corps who oppose the concept of free space. Once we retake Dupliss Region—and we *will* retake it—the same rules will apply to every star within it."

Seeing how the tide of public sentiment was turning in Frontier's favor, Herwin Dirk had begun issuing propaganda of his own. "Veronica Rose is either a cunning liar or a fool," he'd said in his last broadcast. "Those are the only possibilities, since the idea of free space is patently absurd. When the wormhole collapsed, the Dawn Cluster changed forever, and any corp that truly hopes to protect the systems in its care can't afford to let in all comers. Such an approach is a security nightmare—ironic, for a company named Frontier *Security*.

"But in my view, Rose has no intention of ever truly implementing 'free space.' As she's said, she plans to bar her enemies from entering, and when it comes to making enemies, Veronica

Rose casts a wide net. Pay no heed to this lying manipulator. Daybreak will soon bring her to justice, and she will become a footnote in the Dawn Cluster's history."

Listening to those broadcasts, it had struck Thatcher how each CEO was treating the other as the avatar of the company he or she was responsible for. The public was treating them that way, too, along with the CEOs of many other corps. Each one was being presented as the sole mastermind of the corp he led.

That was a fiction, of course. Each CEO's strategy was the work of a team of logisticians and advisers. It was dangerously inaccurate to conflate entire organizations with individuals.

But of course, that's human nature.

So far, Rose's "free space" remained a distant dream. While the two CEOs waged their war of words, the Dawn Cluster's low-security outer zones were transforming from places of open commerce between nations into ones where empires exerted dominance and control over regions. All while the UNC remained in the central cold regions and did nothing.

"Ten minutes to maximum firing range, sir." Grey's voice cut through Thatcher's thoughts. "Wellington is still holding its ground."

Thatcher nodded. "Very good, Ensign." By holding firm against the approaching Frontier ships, Wellington was playing right into their hands. Captain Wilson had known how many ships the opposing corp could field well before entering the system, and he'd brought in a slightly smaller force, to make it more likely that the rogue corp would engage.

Now that they'd clearly chosen to, Frontier would get the footage they needed to make an effective example of the corp.

"I want the *Squall* and the *Incisive* running directional jamming on the three enemy frigates nearest us—the ones bunched together, there. I've already designated them in the holotank." Wilson had let it be known that Thatcher would command any smaller Frontier force the *Jersey* found herself in, and Thatcher had taken that directive at face value. "Tell *Light-foot* to hang back. I want every Alpha Squadron damage dealer to focus on melting down that central frigate with primary lasers."

"Aye, sir. Forwarding your orders now."

Thatcher knew everything he could care to know about Wellington and the composition of its crews. The same went for almost every corp operating out of Dupliss, since Mittelman had taken it upon himself to infiltrate all of them. *Keep your friends close, as they say.*

As a result of that intel, Thatcher knew that the captain of the frigate he'd targeted, the *Contender*, was the least experienced in the company's entire roster, and his crew was even greener.

Frontier beams shot across the void, and the *Contender*'s shields came up a beat too late. She suffered heavy melt on her nose and down along her starboard fore. Even as the force-fields cut off the ravening lasers, something exploded, rupturing the frigate's hull, spewing debris and atmosphere into the void.

The rapid decompression ripped more of her hull away, and then the entire ship went up. With its power source gone, the shield dissipated.

A lucky shot. But one a more experienced opponent would never have allowed Thatcher to take in the first place.

Delta Squadron claimed Frontier's next victim, and then Alpha Squadron's lasers mowed down the shields of the next. This one withstood the attack for ten seconds longer, but in the end her fate was the same as the *Contender*'s.

That was all it took for the Wellington fleet commander to order a ceasefire and initiate a surrender sequence.

Frontier stopped firing the moment they received the surrender. Destroying every last Wellington ship wasn't the sort of example they were looking to make.

Instead, Captain Wilson got on a public channel, so that

everyone in Ramage System could hear him. Thatcher gave Grey the go-ahead to play the transmission for the CIC.

"Wellington Security Solutions." Even addressing an enemy that had just been firing on the ships under his command, Wilson's voice was filled with warmth, like a grandfather admonishing his toddler grandchild. "By falling in with the pirate organization known as Degenerate Empire, you have turned away from every honest person in the Dawn Cluster, spacer and colonist alike. As such, the terms of your surrender are non-negotiable. If you wish to continue doing business, you will do so with your books open to Frontier auditors, who will be free to inspect them at any time, without notice. The same goes for every corp that joined you in consorting with pirates—namely, Skyworks, Corecorp, and Pathways.

"If we find that you are engaging in the practice of charging exorbitant fees to small colonies with no other options and no recourse, you will be shut down. If we find that you have been dragging out contracts for the purpose of inflating the bills you hand to your clients, you will be shut down. If we find you requisitioning local governments for materials we consider unessential for completing a given project, you will be shut down.

"I am Captain Wilson of Frontier Security, commander of the *Triumph*, and I speak with the authority of our CEO, Veronica Rose, who you may know. You can direct your questions and complaints, which I'm confident will be endless, to my primary Ops officer, who will ignore them. Have a nice day."

CHAPTER 6

Redmond, Crystalline Colony
Ramage System, Dupliss Region
Earth Year 2290

ATTACK SHUTTLE ONE SHUDDERED SLIGHTLY AS IT decelerated. Thatcher found himself picturing the segmented wings outside, gradually folding inward to increase air resistance.

Wilson sat strapped in nearby, reading something on his eyepiece, flicking his eyes to scroll through whatever it was. When the shuttle touched down, he turned to smile across the seat separating him from Thatcher. "Ready to enjoy our big welcome?"

Thatcher smiled uncertainly, feeling sure he detected irony in Wilson's voice.

The reason for it became clear the moment they disembarked. One of the governor's aides waited for them outside the airlock, her face dispassionate. Cold, even. When Thatcher met her eyes, she looked away, then seemed to force herself to look at him again.

"Please come with me."

Thatcher exchanged glances with Wilson, who shrugged.

Governor Poirier had requested this meeting—demanded it, if his tone in the recording Thatcher had heard was any indication. He'd assumed the politician's gruffness was just part of his personality. Folk in these far-flung colonies tended to vote for leaders who wore their effectiveness on their sleeves. But the aide's own frigidness suggested Poirier's curtness indicated something else.

The treatment continued as they made their way through the spaceport and into a waiting car outside. The aide sat up with the driver, leaving Thatcher and Wilson sitting across from each other in the back of a stretch speeder.

Wilson was looking at him, a wry grin tugging at the corner of his lips. "Gives you the warm fuzzies, doesn't it?"

Thatcher glanced toward the front of the car, wary of being overheard. He leaned forward slightly and whispered. "Well, I didn't expect parades, but—"

"But to a member of Space Fleet, this comes as something of a shock. Yes?"

Thatcher leaned back. Apparently the former admiral wasn't remotely concerned about being overheard. He nodded.

"I stopped being surprised at receptions like this a long time ago, I'm afraid. These people have been screwed over by PMCs too many times to trust us, even if we do represent a corp with a reputation like Frontier's. Colonists as far out as these are still inclined to assume our company's reputation is a sham. And I can't say I blame them. Startlingly few corps have a conscience. Frontier Security is almost alone in that, and sometimes I worry it will mean the company's doom. That's a big part of why I came out of retirement—to prevent that from happening."

"That's very noble."

Wilson waved a hand. "Oh, please. We both know I don't need any more compliments, and I wasn't fishing for them." The old admiral sighed. "Thatcher, do you ever feel like you've done all this before, many times?"

"Like déjà vu?"

"Yeah."

"Sometimes. I used to feel that way a lot, actually, when I was a boy. But it faded as I grew older."

Wilson gave a small frown, chin crinkling. "When you were a boy? Hmm. And here I thought it was just my age."

The speeder pulled in front of a building, which Thatcher's eyepiece told him was shared by the governor and the Redmond city council. He and Wilson followed the silent aide through the glass double doors and past a series of offices and cubicle farms. At last, they reached a heavy-looking cedar door, which she pulled open, motioning them inside.

Governor Zachariah Poirier's office was small but well-appointed. The walls were lined with sturdy oak bookcases, which held mostly curiosities, impeccably cared for and dusted. There were even a few books scattered here and there. Novelties, at this late date in humanity's development. These were almost certainly printed and bound well after printed books stopped seeing widespread use.

The governor himself sat rigid in a burgundy leather chair, his hands palms-down on the desk. He didn't invite them to sit, but Thatcher followed Wilson's lead in sitting anyway. To do otherwise probably would have been extremely awkward, not to mention insulting, especially to a service member whose career was as storied as Admiral Frederick Wilson's.

Without preamble, Governor Poirier spoke in exactly the same tone he'd used in the message that had prompted this meeting. "What will you do to ensure the safety of the people of Crystalline, now that you've 'liberated' them?"

Wilson and Thatcher both sat with their hands clasped in their laps, blinking at the governor sedately. It occurred to Thatcher that Poirier hadn't mentioned the system's belters living in carved-out asteroids, where everything got recycled for reuse, including their own bodily waste.

I guess even backwater colonists have someone they can ignore and neglect.

One of the governor's hands crept closer, and he used it to rap on the marble desktop, emphasizing his points. "Wellington is no more willing or capable of standing up to the pirates than they were before—less, in fact, with the loss of three of their ships at your hands. And the pirates won't go so easy on Ramage, next time they come here. At least their extortions came in exchange for protection. Safety, of a sort. Frontier Security isn't big enough to sell us your services, even if we wanted to buy them. What's your incentive to protect Ramage?"

Wilson cleared his throat into the silence that ensued. Thatcher had already decided to let him take the lead, here, and the old admiral seemed to sense the governor wasn't finished. That was smart. Better to wait until the tirade had subsided than risk the additional insult of letting the governor interrupt him.

The governor rapped on the desk once more. "You can't go around playing sheriff unless you're actually going to protect the people you impose your brand of law and order on."

Despite his decision not to, Thatcher found himself speaking. "We will protect you."

Wilson glanced at him with a raised eyebrow, but continued to say nothing.

"You say that now," the governor said. "But what will you say once you're in the thick of the war you've picked with Daybreak Combine, your already scant forces stretched thin, with the pirates encroaching from the north?"

Cheeks heating, Thatcher kept his peace, or at least what was left of it. *Fool,* he thought, mostly for himself.

Wilson did speak now, in a voice that was firm and clear. Perhaps he felt that Thatcher had forced his hand. "We're dealing with the pirates. As for your concerns, I promise you I'll take them to Ms. Rose. But you know as well as I do that she plans to retake *all* of Dupliss Region. That's become harder, with things as chaotic as they've become, but once we manage it, Frontier will take care of you just as well as they have the people on Oasis."

The governor snorted, presumably to indicate what he thought of the people on Oasis. "What else can you promise me? Can you promise my people their lives? Can you promise the pirates won't slaughter them in a surprise attack, in retribution for the way you've embarrassed them today?"

Wilson stayed silent, and this time, so did Thatcher. He found himself wondering how effective this Poirier actually was. Could he really have invited them here just to berate them?

The governor continued to glare at Wilson, who didn't flinch. Right then, he looked every inch the admiral, sure of himself even under heavy fire.

"I didn't think so," the governor said.

And with that, the meeting was over.

CHAPTER 7

Aboard the *Triumph*
Windrow System, Dupliss Region
Earth Year 2290

"Bring acceleration up ten percent, Somerton." Wilson cast a sidelong glance at his Helm officer. "At our current speed, the war will be over by the time we reach the jump gate into Pabulum."

Somerton, who could normally be counted on for a chuckle —even at such a low-hanging joke—instead nodded hesitantly before punching the proper commands into his console.

Wilson suppressed the urge to grunt, instead returning his attention to the readout on his own console.

As they sailed through, the Windrow System stayed misleadingly quiet. Misleading, because Wilson's intel told him that on the other side of that jump gate sat the largest force Degenerate Empire had in Dupliss.

Rather, that force was spread across two systems: Pabulum and Agonic. It didn't take an antimatter scientist to figure out why. Together, that pair of systems offered a strategic no-brainer.

Pabulum contained shipyards big enough to service any warship, as long as you didn't count the UNC's super-ships, and Agonic boasted an asteroid belt with enough raw materials to keep the shipyards running for decades—not to mention the regional jump gate into Tempore was located there.

The pirates still didn't have many real warships, but what few they did have seemed to form the backbone of the offensive they'd launched into Dupliss. Both Wilson and Thatcher knew the pirates' campaign had been doomed from the outset. Now they just had to demonstrate that fact to Degenerate Empire's leaders—convincingly enough that they didn't try it again.

Otherwise, we'll have a war on two fronts on our hands, with Daybreak Combine to our west and Degenerate Empire to our north. Everyone knows how those wars tend to shake out.

Wilson frowned at his console, still unsure whether their velocity would take them into Pabulum early enough. A glance around the CIC deepened his frown. "Look alive, people. Just because we have time on our hands isn't an invitation to screw the pooch. It just means projecting more scenarios, and laying in more firing solutions. It means thinking about how the enemy posture might have shifted since our intel was collected—and in what ways that intel might have been flawed."

The way every crewmember instantly became livelier erased Wilson's frown. He knew he normally commanded with a light touch, but that only meant it was more effective when he turned up the heat a degree or two.

"Ops, relay the same orders to the rest of Delta Squadron. I want everyone ready to enter that system with guns blazing, if that's what the situation calls for." He doubted it would. The pirates would likely prove far too covetous of their newly secured shipyards to stray very far from them, so the jump zone would likely be clear.

But it pays to be cautious.

He settled back into the command seat and allowed himself

to enjoy the beehive of activity his little nudge had transformed the CIC into. Rarely did he ever get angry—he could probably count those instances on one hand, across his decades-long military career. But by God, when he did, it got results.

Thinking about that reminded him of Thatcher, whose heavy-handed approach was one of his few shortcomings. Wilson hoped to provide a good example for the young commander, but his hopes weren't high on that score. Thatcher seemed about as stubborn as he was talented.

He refocused on the readout, and made the call inside of two seconds. *We're not going fast enough.* "Give us another fifteen percent, Somerton. Just below cruising speed."

Wilson's XO, Commander Mehta, emitted a fake-sounding cough. He still didn't seem quite used to his new captain's laid-back command style.

His old captain must have been quite the hard ass, considering how reluctant he is to risk talking out of turn. "Speak up, Commander. What's on your mind?"

An instinctive wince tightened Mehta's features before he could compose himself. "Captain, I feel the need to encourage caution, where our acceleration profile is concerned. Given the tactical demands of our present mission, it appears to me that the most prudent action would be to—"

"Good God, Mehta. Spit it out. That's more than enough mealy-mouthed beating around the bush." Wilson delivered the admonishment with a smile, but he really had experienced a flash of irritation as the XO spoke.

"I'm having doubts we can trust Commander Thatcher to reach the Agonic System in time. The pirate forces distributed across Agonic and Pabulum are sizable. If our efforts aren't tightly synchronized, and we allow one enemy force to reinforce the other, then the pirates could win out."

Wilson's eyes narrowed as he studied Mehta's face. Was this an unfiltered assessment, or was it slanted by professional jealousy? If *Triumph* had access to an instant comm unit like the *New Jersey*'s, this wouldn't be an issue in the first place. But while rumor suggested the technology was proliferating faster than the UNC seemed to want, Wilson's destroyer was not yet a beneficiary of it.

To Commander Mehta's credit, he withstood Wilson's scrutiny. Wilson cleared his throat sharply. "What reason do you have to doubt Thatcher's abilities?"

The XO gave a slight shrug. "I understand Commander Thatcher has a reputation for effectiveness, but reputations are often exaggerated. How effective can he really be, if Veronica Rose back-benched him during the assault on Galliot System?"

A couple sharp intakes of air could be heard around the CIC at that remark, and Wilson found himself blinking at his new XO. *The man really is jealous, isn't he?* When he spoke, his tone came out flat—as neutral as he could make it. "I've looked Thatcher in the eye. I've taken his measure. That's all I need to know he's exactly the sort of commander I like to deal with." He took a deep breath, then forced himself to grin. "We proceed under the assumption Thatcher will execute his piece flawlessly. Understood?"

"Yes, sir."

Somerton's hands had been hovering over the Helm console as he waited for the outcome of Wilson's conversation with Mehta. At a final nod from his captain, he resumed tapping at it, initiating the increase in acceleration. As they broke with inertia, a giant's hand gently pressed Wilson back into the seat for a moment, until the inertial compensators kicked back in.

Their new velocity took them across the system in just under six hours. Wilson used the time to grill his CIC crew on several of the possible scenarios that might await them on the other side of the Windrow-Pabulum jump gate.

Before they entered Pabulum, he made them break for an hour, calling second watch to take their places while they rested.

When they returned, they found their captain still in the command seat, working with the second-watch crew to prep the *Triumph* to jump.

"Take us through, Somerton," Wilson said as the first watch Helm officer settled back into his seat. "The course is already laid in, and jump gate readings are all coming back green."

"Aye, sir."

Wilson twisted in the command seat, leaning over the left armrest to briefly lock eyes with his Tactical officer. "Ready, Burkov?"

The Russian nodded, and Wilson felt sure he saw a gleam in his hazel eyes. It was rare to find a Russian working for Frontier Security, given the company's unapologetic American patriotism, as well as the two nations' long-standing rivalry. But Burkov's only goal in life seemed to be getting his mitts on the biggest weapons he could find, regardless of what target fell under his crosshairs. As far as Wilson could judge from his brief tenure aboard the *Triumph,* his colleagues seemed to love him for it.

He didn't need to ask whether the destroyer's four missile tubes were loaded with Hellborns, because they'd seen to that before the break, along with the rest of the battle group.

They'd also decided the order in which Delta Squadron would transition through the jump gate. The battle group's single scout ship went first. With its advanced sensor suite and eWar countermeasures, it would be able to relay the clearest picture to the other ships the moment they entered Pabulum. It would also put the vessel at the greatest risk of being destroyed or disabled, but that was just part of being a scout ship in jump gate warfare.

Wilson's eWar squad went next, interspersed with two of his damage dealers—*Georgia*, a frigate, and *Charger*, a corvette. After that, the rest of his damage dealers transitioned, interspersed with his logistics ships.

It was what might have been called a textbook system entry,

if space warfare had been mature enough to produce a textbook worth the data storage space it took up. Yes, books had been written on the subject, and taught in classrooms, both Space Fleet and corporate. But despite the fact that humanity had built its first space-based warship over a century ago, waging battle in space was something they were still figuring out.

On the one hand, we're fortunate that we haven't had *to figure it out. On the other…it's left us woefully unprepared to fight the Xanthic.*

And to fight each other.

But Wilson chose to look on the bright side. It meant that people like he and Commander Thatcher now enjoyed the opportunity to *write* the rulebook. And the moment their enemies figured out that rulebook, they'd get started on the second edition.

Finally, it was the *Triumph's* turn to transition through the Windrow-Pabulum jump gate. His Ops officer sounded the warning throughout the ship that they were about to pass through.

The three-ringed structure seemed to grip the destroyer the moment she entered the first ring, then flung her across the void. The resulting force shoved Wilson roughly against his seat's back, though it quickly tapered off, with the vessel's state-of-the-art inertial compensators kicking in immediately.

A forty-second interstellar journey took them into the Pabulum System, where their scout ship instantly began sending them the sensor data it had collected.

"It's just as you predicted, sir." His Ops officer, Lieutenant Pete Kelly, continued scrutinizing his console's readout as he relayed the scout's sensor report. "The Degenerate Empire battle group is arrayed around the shipyards, tracking the structure's orbit."

"Acknowledged." Studying the enemy posture on his holoscreen reminded Wilson of his largest-scale engagement during his years fighting pirates in Earth Local Space.

That day, he'd been in a similar position to the one the enemy Degenerate Empire ships found themselves in now—defending a strategically important system against a larger enemy force. Except, unlike them, Wilson had had no expectation of reinforcements. The nearest allied ship had been five systems away.

They'd managed to win the day even so, taking heavy losses in the process. The Degenerate Empire battle group would not enjoy the same success. Like Wilson had been, they were outnumbered. But they also lacked the savvy, skill, and experience Frontier captains and crews had been demonstrating since the collapse of the wormhole connecting Earth to the Dawn Cluster.

What was more, their expectation of reinforcements from Agonic System would make them overconfident. Sloppy.

Unbidden, a smile stretched across Wilson's face.

As they crossed Pabulum toward the enemy, a Degenerate Empire scout ship broke formation with its fellows, headed toward the Pabulum-Agonic jump gate.

Right on cue.

In the long minutes before battle, the pirate ships formed up between the shipyards and the approaching Frontier vessels, taking care to spread out, just as Thatcher's Hellfire barrage tactic had taught them to do.

This time there were no incompetently delayed shields, unlike in Ramage. Clearly, Degenerate Empire had assigned its best commanders to defend Pabulum and Agonic.

Wilson would have to earn his kills, here.

His smile broadened. If he was being honest with himself, that was the way he liked it.

CHAPTER 8

Aboard the *New Jersey*
Empery System, Dupliss Region
Earth Year 2290

ALPHA SQUADRON'S ONLY SCOUT SHIP, THE *CONSTELLATION*, appeared in the jump zone out of Agonic. Her captain wasted no time in transmitting the sensor data she'd collected in the next system.

The Agonic System took shape in the CIC's main holotank, where a transport ship appeared in the scaled-down representation of the jump zone out of Pabulum System. The transport was apparently being used as a scout ship by Degenerate Empire.

Thatcher allowed himself to smile at that. He had high hopes for Frontier's Seer-class scouts, and seeing the cheap toys his enemies were playing with made him all the more eager to realize his vision. Veronica Rose seemed receptive to his ideas, so that was a start. He wanted the upgraded Seers to have eWar capabilities—but incorporating Kibishii stealth tech would be the Holy Grail.

They're not ready to give us that tech yet. But as the tempera-

ture turns up in the Dawn Cluster, corps will realize they can't afford to withhold anything from their allies.

Inside the holotank, the pirate scout ship broadcast an encrypted message throughout the system. The simulation's frame rate was dialed way up, so Thatcher didn't have long to wait before the icons representing the entire Degenerate Empire battle group broke orbit with an inner rocky world and started toward the Agonic-Pabulum jump gate.

"The jump gate into Agonic passed our checks, Captain," Grey volunteered from the Ops station. The man seemed to sense Thatcher's exasperation with him, at least on some level, and had been making an effort to be more proactive. "Alpha Squadron is cleared for system transition." The ensign glanced at Bryce Sullivan, as if waiting for him to start spontaneously astrogating, without an order from his captain.

Thatcher found himself closing his eyes and sighing as silently as could. Grey's overeagerness was just as annoying as his lapses. Both made him miss Guerrero. "We're not transitioning through."

That made the ensign blink, his ruddy cheeks reddening. "C-Captain?"

"We're waiting. Instruct the other Alpha Squadron vessels to do the same."

"Yes, sir." Grey turned to stare at his holoscreen, his body rigid, the very picture of confusion. He relayed the orders, then he sat there, hands fidgeting in his lap.

Ten minutes passed. Twenty. The silence in the CIC was deafening, and so was the coms silence. As always, Thatcher resisted the urge to explain himself to his crew, despite the nervous twitches some of them exhibited. Some—Ortega, Sullivan, and Candle—tapped quietly away at their consoles, preparing their charges for whatever the neighboring system had in store for him. Others shifted anxiously in their chairs, or cast searching looks at colleagues, like Grey did.

This was how a commander maintained authority. The times of greatest uncertainty offered the best opportunities for training his subordinates to trust him, no matter how questionable his decisions seemed on their face.

Once, Grey seemed on the verge of speaking, but one look at Thatcher's face sent him back to an intense study of his holo-screen, which still showed a freeze-frame of the sensor data relayed by the *Constellation.*

Thatcher would have chastised him for not preparing like the others, but luckily for Grey, his main responsibilities included sensors and coms. Nothing of interest was happening in either arena.

At last, Thatcher spoke. "Damage dealers first."

Grey started, as though yanked from a deep reverie.

Thatcher's lips quirked sideways. "The *Jersey* will lead, followed by the rest of our damage dealers. Then eWar, then logistics. Let's move."

Lieutenant Randall Kitt tapped a command into the Helm console, and the light armored cruiser started toward the jump gate, following a course already laid in by Sullivan. It took less than ten minutes for his entire damage dealing squadron to pass through the gate and arrive at the Agonic-side jump zone, then another eight minutes for them to fall into formation according to his instructions.

The other four offensive vessels formed a long, staggered line with the *New Jersey* at their center. A cruiser and a corvette kept pace on the *Jersey*'s starboard side, with a frigate and corvette off their port side.

As soon as the other ships arrived in-system, Thatcher gave the order to cross the system on an intercept course, at top speed. The *Jersey* lurched forward.

His damage dealers would spread out even farther, depending on how the pirate formation responded. At the station to Thatcher's right, his XO gave a satisfied nod. "Your timing was impeccable, sir. We transitioned into the system at the moment when the enemy formation offers the largest possible target. A staggered line rather than the clump they would have been if we'd entered sooner, and engaged them head-on."

"Indeed." The reply seemed terse, even to Thatcher, but he couldn't think what else to say. It wasn't that Candle was wrong—Thatcher's timing had been calculated to give Alpha Squadron the best chance of spreading out and engaging the enemy from multiple angles, coming as close as they could to outright flanking them.

But Candle had been behaving strangely since they'd left Oasis, laying on his flattery even more thickly than usual. Thatcher's grandfather had had a saying for that, as he did for most things. "When they try to feed you honey, watch for the poison."

It was perhaps one of Edward Thatcher's more paranoid sayings, but it was borne of a decades-long military career. Thatcher tried his best to live by the lessons his grandfather's long experience had produced.

Alpha Squadron charged across Agonic System, its eWar and logistics squadrons interspersed behind the damage dealers.

Thatcher turned to Grey. "Have eWar initiate heavy directional sensor jamming. I want the enemy battle group completely blind to what we're doing."

"Aye, sir."

At this stage in Dawn Cluster space warfare, the jamming would be a dead giveaway for what tactic they were using, of course.

"Stand by to forward firing and nav data from Ortega and Sullivan to their counterparts aboard the other damage dealers."

Grey nodded. "Yes, sir."

"Ortega, coordinate with Sullivan, and begin the Hellfire barrage."

Coordinating the barrage was becoming almost second

nature to Frontier Tactical, Nav, Ops, and Helm officers. At Thatcher's suggestion, Rose had had her technicians put together training simulations for drilling the tactic.

Unfortunately, their enemies were also becoming familiar with Hellfire barrages. And so, today would add a new wrinkle or two to the attack.

Thatcher had already discussed that with Ortega, instructing the man not to share those modifications with anyone except the officers who would be involved in executing the attack. Employee rosters in the Dawn Clusters were far too fluid for Thatcher's liking, and playing his cards as tightly to his chest as possible seemed like good OPSEC.

Missiles flew from each of his warship's launch tubes. Then, as one, Alpha Squadron accelerated until they'd almost caught up with their own barrage. With that, they unleashed another wave of Hellborns, which tailed the first, doubling the volley.

They had most of the system's diameter to build up the Hellfire barrage, and Thatcher took full advantage. That was one of his modifications: this would be the largest iteration of the tactic the Dawn Cluster had yet seen.

From the jamming, the Degenerate Empire captains would know Thatcher was executing a Hellfire barrage. But they wouldn't know just how many missiles he was expending.

A pirate adversary wouldn't have been wealthy enough to spend so many Hellborns—Degenerate Empire had not yet established itself enough to afford such an attack.

This effort would prove expensive to Frontier. But Thatcher believed it would pay for itself, in the damage it would prevent to the ships under his command.

Ensign Grey gripped his console as he stared at his holoscreen. When he spoke, his voice thrummed with excitement. "The enemy is spreading out even farther, sir. Most of them have raised shields. I'm assuming the ships who haven't raised them don't have any."

"Acknowledged, Ensign." The pirates had learned to spread out, and these enemies were even competent enough to raise what shields they had in good time.

But Thatcher had another surprise in store for them.

"The first wave of missiles is closing with their targets," Grey said. "They—my God!"

Inside the main holotank, blue beams flashed from the tips of the front-most Hellborns, connecting with the pirates' shields, as well as the exposed hulls of the ships that had raised no force fields.

The missiles were modified Hellborns, of course—modified with laser warheads, designed to soften enemy shields before impact. After encountering their like on the mission to Lacuna, Thatcher had set about acquiring them immediately after returning to Oasis. It had required some digging by Mittelman, and some string-pulling by Rose. But it had gotten done.

Though weakened, every pirate shield survived the laserfire, as well as the first wave of missiles. They withstood the second wave, as well.

That was where the sheer number of missiles Thatcher had fired came into play. The third round caused most of the shields to fail, and the fourth accounted for the rest, along with destroying three smaller ships.

The fifth wave neutralized four more vessels.

Only then did Alpha Squadron close with the enemy, and when they closed, they hit hard. Secondary lasers flashed from turrets mounted on every Frontier ship, the gunners focused on melting the hull of a single corvette, helped by an additional complement of four Hellborns. The corvette ruptured, and at Thatcher's direction, every Frontier damage dealer switched smoothly to the next target, a freighter converted into a light cruiser.

"Transmissions coming in from three different enemy ships,

Captain." Grey twisted in his seat. "They're all saying the same thing. They surrender."

Thatcher pursed his lips, hesitating. He detested the idea of sparing any of his ships to oversee the takeover of the pirate vessels he'd left intact. Almost, he gave the order to simply destroy the remaining pirates.

But he stayed his hand.

For the way they'd terrorized innocent populations throughout Dupliss, the pirates deserved to die. But Thatcher knew that if Frontier gained a reputation for refusing surrender to its foes, then every battle they engaged in would be fought to the bitter end.

Enemies would never admit defeat, knowing they couldn't safely lay down arms against Frontier. The overall cost to the corp would be far greater than the temporary inconvenience Thatcher would endure today. He refused to take the first step toward that grim scenario.

"Ensign, assign the *Lancer* to keep weapons trained on the enemy vessels until we've finished taking them over. Order every Alpha Squadron ship with a marine company to deploy them at once. Major Avery will determine the particulars of the takeovers."

"Aye, sir."

"The moment the attack shuttles have launched, I want every other ship sailing for the Agonic-Pabulum jump gate under full power."

CHAPTER 9

Aboard Attack Shuttle One
Pabulum System, Dupliss Region
Earth Year 2290

PEACE AND QUIET. THAT'S UNUSUAL.

Thatcher had the shuttle's entire passenger compartment to himself for the short trip between the *Jersey* and the *Triumph*. A rare moment of solitude.

He experienced some light jostling as the dock's twin arms extended, long and spindly, to lift the shuttle from its cradle on the cruiser's port side and then position it in space, several meters away from the warship's hull. The arms were powerful enough to fling the shuttle away at high speed, for a combat launch, but luckily that wouldn't be necessary today.

The pilot engaged the shuttle's thrusters, and Thatcher swayed slightly to the right as the craft came about to point at its destination. Then it accelerated forward, and the inertial compensators soon made it feel as though they weren't moving at all.

Thatcher crossed his arms and reflected on the engagement that had ended two hours ago. After Agonic, Pabulum had been a cakewalk. Wilson's Delta Squadron had held strong, and together both forces had outflanked the remaining pirate vessels brutally, eliciting a quick surrender and winning Frontier seven new ships, to go with the five Alpha Squadron had captured in Agonic System.

He should be focused on the total rout he and Wilson had pulled off. Instead, he couldn't stop thinking about the loss of the *Georgia*, which the pirates had managed to isolate and destroy just before Thatcher's arrival.

If I'd been just a little faster…

Casualties had been minimal, as much of the ship was still intact, and most of the crew had evacuated safely. But the frigate's ability to maneuver was gone, and the damage was well beyond what repair drones could do. Frontier could send out repair crews, try to reclaim her…but what were the chances she'd still be here by the time they arrived? More likely, scavengers would claim her first. Probably Degenerate Empire itself would…if they dared set foot in Dupliss again.

There's that to be grateful for, at least. The back of the so-called Empire's presence in Dupliss was now broken. Hopefully, it was so badly broken that they'd hesitate to return anytime soon.

Something still nagged at him, though. During his voyage to investigate Xanthic activity in Lacuna, he'd had to detour around Nankeen System, as the pirates had locked that system down. They'd seemed determined to prevent anyone from entering it— so determined that the ships guarding the system's entrance hadn't abandoned their posts even to pursue the Frontier battle group penetrating deep inside their territory.

What were they hiding there? What could be so important to them?

Thatcher shook his head to clear it, forcing himself to enjoy the peaceful solitude of the shuttle ride. He was en route to see Captain Wilson, who'd insisted they meet in-person in order to perform what he called a "postmortem" on the battle they'd just waged.

"You might not be familiar with the tradition, since you were never a captain with Space Fleet." Wilson had winked at him from the holoscreen built into Thatcher's desk. "'Postmortem' is code for using our win as an excuse to crack open the bottle of Japanese whiskey I've been keeping for just such an occasion."

Attack Shuttle One docked on the *Triumph*'s starboard side, and Thatcher ordered the pilot—a lieutenant named Brin Hodge, call sign Hotdog—to remain until he returned.

As he walked from the shuttle dock to Wilson's office, guided by instructions that downloaded automatically onto his comm, Thatcher noted something he'd initially noticed his first time aboard the destroyer.

The passageways weren't as immaculate as those aboard the *Jersey*, but they weren't dirty, either. What was more, the crewmembers he passed seemed more…jovial…than he was used to. More enthusiastic.

It occurred to him that enthusiasm might be more useful to a warship's effectiveness than the constant striving for perfection he'd managed to instill in his own crew. He wasn't totally sold on that possibility, but it *was* certainly pleasant to spend time aboard the *Triumph*. A more enjoyable experience didn't necessarily equate to enhanced military prowess, but it did perhaps open him slightly to the idea.

"Sir?"

Thatcher turned toward the man who'd spoken, now paused in the process of emerging into the corridor from a side hatch. A young-looking officer, he wore the golden 'butterbars' of an ensign on the shoulder epaulets of his working uniform. "Yes, Ensign?"

"If I could have just a moment of your time…"

Coming to a full stop, Thatcher nodded. "Go ahead."

"I want to thank you, sir. For what you've done for Frontier.

The company's reputation, and the overall culture…I'm not sure you're aware of this, sir, but you've been an inspiration to a lot of us."

Thatcher blinked at the officer, dumbfounded. "I was merely doing my duty."

The ensign smiled. "I know. But it's the *way* you did it that made the difference. It kept more of us alive than you may realize. So thank you. But I won't keep you any more. I assume you're here to see Captain Wilson—you know the way?"

"Yes," Thatcher said with a nod, gesturing with his comm.

"Very good. By your leave, sir."

"Dismissed."

The ensign walked off down the passageway, the way Thatcher had come. The man had an evident bounce in his step.

Shaking himself, Thatcher turned to continue on his way.

The conversation left him feeling conflicted as he returned to his previous train of thought. On one hand, he couldn't recall having any encounters like that aboard the *New Jersey.* Instead, *he* was the one to always seek out crewmembers, to ask about their experience aboard the ship, and in doing so to take the measure of his ship's health.

But his crew rarely approached *him,* and certainly not to deliver such praise.

Had he forged the relationship with his crew that he thought he had?

On the other hand, if the ensign believes I deserve that level of praise, I must be doing something right.

He reached Wilson's office, and was admitted at a knock. The former admiral waved away his salute. "At ease, Tad. Take a seat."

As Thatcher sat, Wilson was already cracking open the whiskey. He proceeded to pour about a shot each for them into the bottom of two glasses. "Ice?"

"No, thank you."

"Good man."

Wilson slid Thatcher's glass to him, and he took it. They each raised their glasses to each other, then took their first sips.

Thatcher swirled his mouthful around. *Is that…?* He nodded to himself. *Hint of butterscotch.* "I have to admit to feeling a little bad about drinking whiskey while my crew works to make the *Jersey* ready for the return trip."

His host gestured dismissively with his hand holding the glass. "Commanders are human too, Tad. We have to remember that, even if everyone else tends to forget. If we don't take at least a little time for ourselves, our batteries will never get the chance to recharge. Which means it'll be impossible to run on full power when you need to most."

"Still. It feels…odd."

"Isn't your XO competent?"

"Well, yes."

"Then relax. Now *that's* an order."

Thatcher forced himself to smile. He still found it challenging to fully relax in the presence of his childhood hero.

"Tell me about your family," Wilson said. "You're married?"

Thatcher nodded, thinking of Lin. Her beautiful brown eyes staring up into his. The way her slender body fit snugly into his when they lay together in bed. A deep ache arose in his stomach, and he chased it with another sip of whiskey.

"You miss her?"

"With every fiber of my being. We're expecting. A boy."

Wilson nodded, studying Thatcher, his expression grown serious.

Thatcher took another sip, too soon, and the alcohol burned as it went down. He took another. "Her photo is the first thing I see every morning, and the last thing before I fall asleep. She's why I strive as hard as I can to out-think the enemy. To be better than them—whether it's Reardon Interstellar, the Xanthic, or

Degenerate Empire. We *have* to unite the Dawn Cluster. And we have to return to Earth Local Space in force."

"To oust the aliens."

"Not just oust them. Crush them. So that they'll never threaten us again." Thatcher took a long pull from his glass, and found it was empty. He set it on Wilson's desk with a thunk. Suddenly, he wanted to be back on the *Jersey*, in the command seat. To oversee preparations for getting underway—to make sure they finished them as quickly as possible. So that they could get back to Freedom, and win this war. So Thatcher could get to figuring out a way home.

Wilson was frowning, now. "This didn't work, did it? You're not relaxing."

At that moment, Thatcher's comm buzzed. He removed it from its holster and placed it on the desk, in speaker mode.

"Captain. Bill Candle here."

"Go ahead, Lieu—uh, Bill."

"We've just received word via instant comm that the Daybreak Combine is amassing forces in the Splay, along Dupliss' western border. Ms. Rose requires our presence in Freedom System as soon as we can manage."

"Thank you, Bill. I'm coming back over to the *Jersey* now."

Before he rose to leave, Thatcher's eyes met his host's across the desk.

Wilson sighed. "Maybe our opportunities to relax are all well behind us."

CHAPTER 10

New Houston, Oasis Colony
Freedom System, Dupliss Region
Earth Year 2290

*C*HRISTMAS DECORATIONS.

Garland lined the walls in the waiting room outside Veronica Rose's office, and a handsome wreath adorned the oak door behind which Thatcher knew Rose worked, keeping him waiting. A gleaming crimson bow drooped from the bottom of the wreath's circle.

I completely forgot about Christmas.

He knew what date it was, of course—December 4th, making Christmas Day exactly three weeks away. His thoughts were simply occupied by other matters.

Pirates. Daybreak Combine. The looming threat of the Xanthic returning, at any moment.

He hadn't given the matter of Christmas any actual thought, but now that he did, he realized he'd subconsciously assumed that the holiday would be canceled until something like normality resumed for humanity.

She's keeping me waiting. That was clear. The real question was why.

Hadn't it been enough to backbench him while the *Jersey* underwent repairs, without even raising the possibility of giving him another command in the meantime, despite his accomplishments since arriving in the Dawn Cluster?

Had it not been sufficient to take away command of a battle group, and place him under Wilson instead?

Apparently not. Rose also chose to subject him to the indignity of making him wait, for over ten minutes now.

The door opened, at last, and Rose herself stuck her head out. "Commander. Please, come in."

That was somewhat unexpected. Usually, Rose would have signaled the receptionist electronically that she was ready to receive the waiting room's next occupant. The fact that she personally held the door for him seemed to contradict her decision to make him languish out here.

As he brushed past her, he breathed in her usual lilac scent. Unbidden, a sense of calm washed over him, muting the conflicting emotions he'd been experiencing out in the reception area.

How was she able to do that to him? Guilt twinged from the back of his mind at the pleasure he took from being in her company.

He cleared his throat as he took the seat facing Rose's desk, then realized he likely should have waited for permission to sit. It was what one of his own subordinates would have done—and Rose was, in a sense, a captain in her own right. The captain of Frontier Security.

She didn't remark on his lapse, crossing the room to circle the desk in silence.

The look she gave him after settling into her chair confounded him. It looked equal parts inviting and irritated.

How am I to act around this woman?

And why have I completely forgotten how?

"How is Guerrero?" he asked.

The question dispelled the moment, and Rose's usual poise returned.

"She's recovering. Slowly." Rose pursed her lips, forming a bud of scarlet in her otherwise pale face. "It will be some time before she's fit for duty, I'm afraid, Commander."

Thatcher lowered his gaze to the desk's bottom edge and said nothing.

"You look ashamed."

His gaze jerked back up at the frankness of the comment. "I am. I ruined a perfectly good officer." He forced himself to take a deep breath. *If she's going to be so frank, then I suppose I can, too.* "Is that why you benched me, for a time? And put me under Admiral Wilson's command afterward?"

Rose chuckled, though the sound held little mirth. "You're nothing if not candid, are you, Commander?"

I could say the same about you. But he decided to keep the remark to himself.

She shook her head. "There are a number of reasons I decided you needed a break. Either way, that break has ended. War, as you know, is upon us. And we find ourselves woefully outnumbered."

"How far along are we with the nanofab tech?"

"Not very. Having the technology is one thing, actually implementing it quite another. We not only have to build the nanofab facilities themselves, but we have to do it without the UNC noticing. Of course, they'll notice eventually, and by the time they do we need to have constructed a fleet so large that it doesn't matter whether they know or not. That way, no one can take it from us. So we also have to figure out how to hide the fleet as we build it."

Thatcher nodded. "And then there's the issue you haven't raised."

The Frontier CEO raised her eyebrows.

"The fact we got the tech from a Xanthic terminal," he said. "That concerns me. A lot."

Rose furrowed her brow. "You don't think they predicted we would recover the terminal from that cave on Recept, do you? If they're that prescient, I expect we're all doomed."

"No. I only mean that they obviously have the technology as well."

"Right. I've thought about that, too. The part I can't understand is, if they have nanofabbers, why are they limiting themselves to ground assaults? Aside from the battle over Recept, I mean."

"They can't have had the technology for long, else I'm sure we'd be dead already. But they'll be building their own secret fleet, I'm sure."

"Yet another problem for Frontier to deal with."

Thatcher wished he could disagree with her there. Except, the rest of the Dawn Cluster seemed too embroiled in their own wars to bother much with the Xanthic. Only Frontier seemed willing to attempt it while waging a war of its own.

And even our attempt is looking fairly grim, at present. "Speaking of the engagement over Recept…have you made any progress with finding out how it came to be that we fought the same Xanthic warships my grandfather did?"

"Yes, actually."

He inclined his head, and waited.

"Are you familiar with the Novikov self-consistency principle?" she asked.

"No."

"Consistent causal time loops?"

He shook his head. "They didn't cover that at the academy."

"Imagine a billiard ball knocked into a wormhole—but not the sort of wormhole that connected the Dawn Cluster with Earth Local Space. Instead, this wormhole bridges periods of time, sending the billiard ball into the past, where it collides with itself. But the ball emerges from the future at a different angle, delivering a glancing blow to its past self. This blow changes its trajectory to exactly the right degree for it to emerge in the past at just the right angle to deliver the same glancing blow."

"What do billiard balls have to do with the Xanthic fleet we faced?"

"It follows the same principle. If we hadn't diminished the fleet as we had, then humanity likely would have lost to the Xanthic fifty years ago. Meaning we never would have colonized the Dawn Cluster, and our battle group never would have been able to diminish their attacking fleet. It seems Novikov was right about time travel. It abhors a paradox, just as nature abhors a vacuum."

Thatcher found himself slowly shaking his head back and forth, and he stopped himself. He didn't know how to contend with what Rose had just told him. What were the strategic implications? Were there any?

He decided to change the subject to something he could understand. "Where along the Dupliss-Splay border do you intend to deploy the *New Jersey*?"

"You aren't going to the border."

He narrowed his eyes. "Pardon?"

"I said, you aren't going to the border, Commander. You're going to find Captain Moll."

Thatcher schooled his face to neutrality, in an attempt to suppress the revulsion that threatened to surface there. "Moll."

"Yes. He's said nothing on the record about Daybreak aligning itself with pirates, and now he's fallen completely out of touch. I have to believe he doesn't support Herwin Dirk. And we can't win this thing without him. So the *Jersey* will search for him. You'll have the authority to negotiate with him on my behalf. Or with someone who has equivalent authority, though somehow I doubt Moll would vest anyone with that."

"Where will I be conducting this search?" Noticing he'd stiffened in his seat, Thatcher tried to make himself relax.

"Apparently no one in Candor knows where he is. Or at least, if they do, they're pretending not to. Still, you might begin your search there. Maybe someone saw him leaving Sunder HQ, and can at least tell you which direction he went."

Thatcher wanted to put his face in his hands. The idea of being away from the front lines of the war with Daybreak made him itch. He realized how important the mission was that Rose had given him, but still…he considered himself an odd choice to conduct diplomacy with Moll.

Maybe this is her idea of continuing to teach me humility. Or something. Maybe Rose wasn't done punishing him, after all.

It didn't matter. She was his superior, and he would follow orders.

"Very well."

Rose nodded, in a way that made it clear he was dismissed.

But before he could leave, she spoke again. "Have you planned anything for your crew, to celebrate Christmas, Commander?"

He paused with his hand resting on the great door's handle and met her eyes over his shoulder. "I haven't given it any thought."

She gave him a smile that looked sad, and somewhat disappointed. His stomach dropped a little, at that.

"You're dismissed, Commander."

CHAPTER 11

New Houston, Oasis Colony
Freedom System, Dupliss Region
Earth Year 2290

THE MOMENT TAD LEFT HER OFFICE, ROSE SAGGED IN HER SEAT and stared up at the smooth, white ceiling.

The effort it took to constantly keep him at arm's length exacted a toll unexpected in its size. Throughout the meeting, she'd forced herself to call him "Commander," not "Tad," as she'd grown used to doing. And she'd tried her best to treat him as a somewhat unruly subordinate, which he was.

But he was more than that. She'd let him think that the reason for "benching" him, as he put it, mostly had to do with Guerrero, but that was false.

There was a much bigger reason, one that threatened to severely compromise her judgment. A reason she had finally acknowledged, if only to herself.

I love him. I love Tad Thatcher.

God help her. Everything about it was wrong—the fact that he was her subordinate, and her best captain. She needed to wield him like a weapon against Frontier's enemies, and her feelings for him had no place in that.

They persisted all the same. His sheer competence was part of it. It had caught her heart's attention, anyway. But his constancy, and his firmness, had captured it. The way his dark brown eyes locked onto hers, as if boring into her soul…

A thrill ran through her, and she shivered.

Get control of yourself.

Mittelman had picked up on something. She wasn't sure how deeply the spymaster saw, but he'd seen fit to tell her she relied too much on the commander.

And he was right. That was why she'd chosen to send the man far away. It was best for everyone, right now. Most importantly, it was best for Frontier.

His mission would likely involve trekking through some dangerous territory, and it didn't amount to a misuse of his skill. Indeed, victory in the war with Daybreak Combine likely hinged on finding Moll, so it made sense to send her best captain.

It also reduced the risk of her compromising her judgment as much as possible.

For now, anyway. Until he returns.

She drew a deep breath, sitting straighter in her chair. Exhaustion threatened to crash over her, to send her trudging toward her chambers, but she fought it back.

For now, they had no idea where Moll was, and she had to do what she could for her company, and for the people of Oasis— for the people of Freedom System, and of all Dupliss.

For the entire Dawn Cluster. Life under Herwin Dirk, the sort of man without qualms about siding with pirates, would not be pleasant for anyone. She would fight to avoid that at all costs.

Rose had no doubt that conquering the Dawn Cluster was his ultimate goal. If Dirk defeated Frontier, then between Daybreak and their pirate allies, he would control the entire north. After that, he likely expected the rest of the Cluster would fall into his hands, especially with the south warring against itself.

Activating her desk-mounted camera, she checked her appearance, brushing a stray strand of black hair away from her eyes. In the holoscreen, she looked tired but determined. That would do.

In the fight against Dirk, she didn't have his vast fleets. But she had words. And as Simon Moll had rightly predicted, words were quickly becoming the most powerful ammunition in the Cluster.

"People of the Dawn Cluster," she said to the camera, "I come to you with news that should warm the hearts of every righteous man and woman on this side of the galaxy. Frontier captains Frederick Wilson and Tad Thatcher have recently returned from the mission I gave them: to throw the vile Degenerate Empire back from whence they came."

She suppressed the urge to grimace at her use of the archaic word "whence." But between Mittelman's intel and focus testing conducted by Frontier media specialists, she'd learned that the somewhat grandiose parts of her broadcasts were what had resonated most with her audience, whether they were civilians or military firm employees.

Her inclination toward verbosity was becoming an important part of her brand, so she'd decided to use that. It both pleased her admirers and infuriated her detractors. That was enough to get her to start playing it up.

"What pirate ships we didn't destroy, we sent fleeing back into Tempore Region. And we did it with minimal losses. Let the Degenerate Empire cower, lick their wounds, and reflect on what happened to them when they attempted to carry out their dark agenda. Let this be a lesson to any pirate throughout the Cluster who would seek to impinge on the rights and freedoms of free peoples. Corps like Frontier Security and our allies will not stand for it. Your behavior is not sustainable—not as long as there are companies willing to act as beacons of justice—as shining upholders of what is right."

She spoke with a level of confidence she knew she had no true claim to, considering how desperate Frontier's position was in view of the upcoming war. Her only hope was to pretend that it wasn't the case. She aimed her words like an arrow, with the hearts and minds of the Cluster's residents as her target.

Would Frontier's success in throwing back the pirates sway more corps into becoming much-needed allies? It would probably help, but she doubted it would be enough by itself.

She needed to paint an even grander picture.

"The Dupliss Region has once again become one of free space—a concept that has become necessary in this climate of chaos and, let's face it, lawlessness. Without hope of UNC fleets swooping in to establish order, those corps who place the public good on equal footing with profit have a duty to the people that live here. We must establish and maintain free space throughout this Cluster. Civil liberties, and freedom, must be upheld. No man or woman's speech must be curtailed, and no one should be coerced into acting against their interests. Further, any ship at all can pass freely though free space, so long as they mean no harm. There are those who believe implementing free space will weaken us, but nothing could be more wrong. It will only strengthen the ties between right-thinking corps, making us all safer. So let commerce flow freely, and let the strong protect those who cannot protect themselves.

"I honor those corps who work to uphold freedom throughout the Dawn Cluster. But I say emphatically: shame on those who will not. Right now, Frontier Security has become a focal point in the fight for freedom, and at present, doing what is right means helping us to defeat Herwin Dirk and his Combine. They have shown themselves willing to sell the freedom of this Cluster's people to pirates. And they ignore the greater threat that lurks on the Cluster's edges—the Xanthic, who have come to attack us even here, in this far-flung home humanity has made for itself across the galaxy.

"I refuse to stand for the Combine's malfeasance. And I pray that you won't, either."

She ended the broadcast, then sat quietly for a moment, wondering whether it would be enough. Going over the words she'd spoken, they seemed cheap, and inadequate. But she often felt that way about her broadcasts after she conducted them. She'd learned that her personal feelings about them had little to do with how the Cluster's public would receive them.

If her other broadcasts were any indication, this one would have the desired effect.

Which was good. Because it was challenging to reconcile an image of righteousness with fierceness in war.

Not impossible, but challenging.

And she was about to do something that would make her look fierce indeed.

CHAPTER 12

Aboard the *Triumph*
Laniferous System, The Splay
Earth Year 2290

"Approaching the Laniferous-Schesis jump gate now, Captain. Gate checks are coming back yellow."

Wilson narrowed his eyes at the Ops officer. "Yellow?"

Kelly nodded. "The gate underwent maintenance recently, after a barge came out the other end missing a large section of her port-side hull. The gate's been functioning without issue since the repairs, but the crew who performed them needs to perform one last inspection before its rating gets bumped back up to green."

Air left Wilson's lungs in a slow exhale. *That shouldn't interfere with the mission.* He felt safe enough using the gate, but the fact no one had alerted him to its yellow status annoyed him. *How did Mittelman's spies miss that one?* "Confirm to the other ships that we're transitioning immediately. EWar first."

"Aye, sir." The lieutenant gave him an odd look as he said it, and Wilson realized he'd forgotten to use the new system for issuing inter-ship orders.

Damn it. He'd been trying to get the other crews accustomed to the new system, and forgetting to use it didn't help with that.

Wilson watched his holoscreen as the compact eWar ship slipped into the first ring, then became an elongated beam of light and vanished. The *Andrew* jumped next—a frigate they'd liberated during their raid on Freya Station.

They'd spent the last several hours transitioning through Laniferous, a system on The Splay's eastern border with Dupliss, and one Herwin Dirk thought was firmly in his grasp.

Not so much. Not anymore, at any rate.

Rose's broadcast had had a swift and significant impact throughout the Cluster, including on the corps in this very system. Before, they'd been silent about Daybreak's transgressions, which gave the impression they condoned them.

But Rose's words had shamed them into letting Wilson's strike force pass quietly through their system. The corps here had apparently decided they didn't want history to remember them as complicit with pirates.

Another effect of the broadcast had been to alert the rest of the Cluster to exactly how big the war in the north might become.

One of the first things corps had done following the collapse of the wormhole to Earth was to start forming alliances, in order to fill the sudden security vacuum. If the Northern War, as many had taken to calling it, happened to spill outside the many regions it had already engulfed, it could set off a cascade of mutual defense agreements that would embroil the entire Cluster in the fighting.

In the south, warring alliances on all sides—and even those not currently fighting, many of which had portrayed themselves as neutral until now—had begun broadcasting warnings, one after another, that if their territories or that of their allies were to come under attack, they would immediately join the war on the side of Frontier Security.

They see Daybreak as the aggressor. No one thinks Frontier or our allies will attack them.

That was worth something. But other than Kibishii, no PMCs had yet come out fully in support of Veronica Rose's corp.

So we have to show them this war is winnable.

The *Triumph*'s turn came to transition, the gate flinging the destroyer across the void and into Schesis System. Once there, he gave the order to head to their final destination: a major mineral refinery in the system's asteroid belt. He remembered to use the new comm system for distributing orders this time, speaking the order himself over a battle group-wide channel rather than relaying it through his Ops officer. The channel would deliver his voice to the CIC of each ship—the first step toward realizing Tad Thatcher's vision of wholly integrating the CICs of any given force, making it a more cohesive, efficient unit.

Wilson supported that vision with enthusiasm. The new way of doing things would see Nav officers linking their consoles with their counterparts aboard other ships, speeding up the entire group's astrogation. Ops officers would share sensor data, and Tactical officers their firing solutions, along with helping each other spot calculation errors.

There was a lot of pushback, as was always the case with something so new. For that reason, Veronica Rose had insisted they roll out the new system slowly. Piecemeal.

But they all agreed it would give every Frontier force, large or small, greater versatility and effectiveness. They'd be able to respond to changing battlespace conditions faster than their enemies.

At least, until those enemies figure out what we're doing, and copy us. Then we'll have to move on to the next innovation.

Wilson cast his gaze from officer to officer. The good cheer that usually filled his CIC was gone. The mood was deadly serious, today.

The battle group he commanded was as lean as he could make it while meeting their needs, both to minimize the chances of detection and to leave as many ships protecting the home front as possible. His force consisted of four vessels: the eWar and logistics ships, plus the *Triumph* and the *Andrew*. By now, two platoons' worth of marines would be waiting in attack shuttles docked along the *Triumph*'s starboard side, already in pressure suits and fully kitted out.

Wilson felt no shame in admitting he'd been studying Thatcher's playbook closely, and he took satisfaction in the knowledge he'd adapted it neatly for the current situation.

A traditional approach would have had his destroyer filling the role of primary damage dealer, with the frigate playing support. And because that was established tradition, any serious effort at defending the mineral refinery would target the destroyer first.

But Wilson didn't plan to deal much damage with the *Triumph* today. Instead, he'd had almost every weapons module in the vessel stripped out, and replaced with additional capacitor power.

Paired with the logistics ship feeding her power via microwave beam, the destroyer's shields were likely capable of holding against up to four attacking warships. Against the lone cruiser currently protecting the refinery, it would be virtually impenetrable. Even when you added in the refinery's complement of swivel-mounted railguns.

Meanwhile, almost all of the *Andrew*'s capacitors had been replaced with extra missile bays, all stuffed full with high-yield Hellborns. Some capacitor power had been left to her, to allow her to raise shields long enough to escape in the event the enemy somehow figured out what Wilson had done in time to target the frigate. But if that happened, he would be very surprised.

In the two hours it took to reach the refinery, the armored cruiser guarding it sent out a series of encrypted transmissions, at shorter and shorter intervals.

Her captain's getting frantic. It was the only Daybreak warship in-system, and it didn't take a genius to guess the contents of those messages: requests for one of the various private mining vessels, freighters, and transports in the system to carry a request for backup to the neighboring system. But no one seemed to want to help.

Wilson caught himself grinning, and he schooled his face to seriousness. *Maybe there are more corps on our side than we think. They're just too scared of Daybreak to make it known.*

Whatever the case, Wilson had caught Herwin Dirk with his pants down. The man clearly hadn't expected Frontier to gain such easy access to the Schesis refinery, which served almost half of The Splay's systems. It also happened to be the last refinery of any size owned by Dirk's corp, Paragon Industries. Paragon's mining arm had grown fairly small since its transformation from a mining corp into one that principally ran security for other mining companies.

Maybe Dirk doesn't think a Frontier commander would be morally capable of doing what I'm about to.

As expected, the cruiser targeted the *Triumph* once she was within firing range, and so did the refinery's turrets, letting loose with solid-core rounds from the railguns while lasers lanced out from every one of the cruiser's gun ports facing the destroyer.

Wilson watched the shield readout on his holoscreen with grim satisfaction. His forcefield's power was ticking down by mere hundredths of a percentage. "Return fire with our primary laser."

"Aye," Burkov said, and seconds later the beam shot out to connect with the cruiser's own shield, which immediately began to shimmer.

As the enemy hammered away with everything they had at

the *Triumph*'s shields, the *Andrew* sailed forward unchallenged, until she reached a proximity with the cruiser that two opposing warships rarely ever achieved.

With that, the *Andrew* launched a stream of Hellborns, feeding them straight into the cruiser's starboard side.

There was barely any time for the enemy captain to react. The first missile caused the cruiser's shield to shudder and buck wildly, and the second dropped it. The next opened up a section of her hull. And the fourth and fifth Hellborns bit deep into her guts.

An explosion of fiery debris was the result.

The cruiser destroyed, the *Andrew* turned its attention to the refinery, assigning two missiles each to the turrets facing her.

Near the end, a few of the remaining turrets targeted the Frontier frigate, but she raised her shield without flinching. The logistics ship switched from bolstering the *Triumph*'s shield to charging the *Andrew*'s, keeping it intact long enough to deal with the remaining turrets.

Wilson tapped at his console to open up a channel with his marine commander. "Time to deploy, Major."

"Yes, sir."

Twin shudders ran through the CIC, barely noticeable. The attack shuttles launching.

Less than twenty minutes after the marines boarded the refinery, a civilian transport decoupled with the structure, departing at full speed. Five minutes later, another one followed suit.

The marine commander spoke into Wilson's ear. "That's everyone, sir. We're coming back now."

"Excellent. Tell your boys good work." He switched over to a channel that gave him direct access to the *Andrew*'s CIC.

"Captain Conroy. Kindly reduce that refinery to rubble."

"With pleasure."

Yet another barrage of Hellborns streamed out of the frigate toward the unshielded mineral refinery. It took nine to finish it off—the many volatile compounds aboard the station no doubt helped to trigger the cascading explosion.

Wilson spoke once more over the group-wide channel. "That's our work done, then. Let's take our leave, before Dirk sends some sort of welcoming party."

The Frontier ships about-faced unceremoniously, accelerating back toward the jump gate into Laniferous.

He knew his actions today would compromise Frontier's moral superiority somewhat, and Rose knew it, too. But they had to hamstring the massive Daybreak war machine somehow.

Today's success should achieve some effect in that regard, especially combined with their recent pillaging of Freya Station.

We have a lot left to do before we gain a hope of winning. Dirk will be geared up for war all too soon.

Optics had held them back from destroying Freya Station outright, during their attack on Galliot System.

Not today. Destroying the mineral refinery had been a calculated risk. They'd needed to demonstrate strength to the Cluster's other corps—to make them start believing Frontier's cause wasn't a pipe dream.

There was also a slight difference between the refinery and Freya Station, beyond the obvious. The station had been jointly owned by Meridian and Paragon Industries. Less of Meridian's dirty work had come to light than Paragon's, so it had less mud on its face.

Destroying a facility that Meridian had an ownership stake in would have been seen as excessive aggression. But destroying the last major refinery Paragon owned…that would play a lot better with the Dawn Cluster's public.

CHAPTER 13

UNC Headquarters on Planet Bimaria
Sunrise System, Clime Region
Earth Year 2290

THATCHER PAUSED MID-STRIDE AND COCKED HIS HEAD.

They were playing Herwin Dirk's propaganda through the corridor's overhead speakers.

He crossed his arms and stood in the middle of the hallway, frowning as he listened to the leader of the Daybreak superalliance respond to Frontier's attack on the Paragon mineral refinery.

"Is this what she means by 'free space?' That Frontier Security is free to pillage and burn its way through any space Veronica Rose wishes? That's what I call a dark vision for the Dawn Cluster. The Frontier CEO is nothing but a pompous liar. We heed her at her peril."

Shaking his head, Thatcher continued on his way. *Do they play Rose's propaganda in equal measure, here?* Perhaps they did. Thatcher supposed the UNC was keeping a close eye on what was happening throughout the Cluster. Things could turn on a dime, and already had, at least a couple times since the wormhole to Earth Local Space had closed. With access to most of the UNC fleet now cut off, what personnel were still here needed to remain nimble. Ready for anything.

And he was here to aid them in that, God help him.

His eyepiece flashed, indicating that he'd arrived at the office of the UNC Deputy Chief of Operations for the Dawn Cluster. He turned to face the door, which promptly slid open for him. He entered into a well-appointed waiting room, where the walls were adorned with carefully non-denominational holiday decorations.

"Commander Thatcher." The receptionist smiled warmly from her desk. A cup full of candy canes sat next to her left elbow. "Please have a seat." Slender, red-tipped fingers stretched toward an empty chair directly across from the desk. "The Deputy Chief will receive you shortly."

Thatcher grunted, and sat.

The scarlet, long-haired rug beneath his service boots seemed out of place for a public official's office. He studied it with a frown, though he was fairly certain the frown itself was left over from hearing Dirk's broadcast.

He wondered if Rose had expected the man's counter-propaganda to be quite so effective. Dirk wasn't known for a way with words, but it seemed he'd hired on some skilled PR folks. His messaging was getting spikier.

I imagine he'll sway some people. Rose already had her detractors, after all.

Thinking of Rose made him wonder what she would say if she knew he was here, right now.

Nothing good. That conversation would be full of yelling, possibly followed by his termination.

The regions he was taking the *Jersey* through were the only ones that led to Sunder's HQ in Candor Region without traveling through enemy territory or going the long way through a wartorn star cluster.

His route made sense…except that this detour to Sunrise System, the system that had once held the wormhole to Earth, had not been needed. In fact, it had cost him time.

None of his crew knew why he was here, nor did they question him. Likely, they assumed it involved secret orders from Veronica Rose. Nothing could be further from the truth.

When they'd first entered Sunrise, Candle had remarked on how different the system looked since the last time they'd visited. Back then, shortly after the wormhole's collapse, Sunrise had been crawling with traffic, most of it clustered around UNC facilities, waiting for an audience with an official so they could air their grievances and make their demands. Since then, it had become clear that in a post-wormhole Cluster, the United Nations and Colonies were entertaining neither.

Now, there was less than a tenth of the ships in Sunrise than there'd been during his last visit. There were even fewer UNC super-ships. Their greater presence before had likely been for security reasons.

The various nation-owned space stations followed their lonely orbits, with almost no vessels traveling between them, and just as little comm chatter. The tension was palpable, even across the great, breathless void.

Thatcher cast his thoughts further back, to when he'd entered the Dawn Cluster for the first time. Things had been more or less normal here then, other than the news that Earth Local Space was under attack again by the Xanthic.

He remembered his worry about Lin evacuating to the moon with her parents. Even more vividly, he remembered the anticipation of their son's birth, and the sincere belief he would see his wife again soon.

He prayed every night that they were safe. These days, the

not knowing filled what little sleep he managed to get with nightmares. And the nightmares were getting worse.

He caught himself rubbing his eyes, and stopped.

"Commander Thatcher?"

He looked up to find the receptionist's easy smile unchanged. Apparently she was used to wearing it for irritable guests who didn't talk.

"The Deputy Chief will see you, now." As she finished her sentence, a great pine slab of a door swung open ominously to Thatcher's left.

"Thank you," he said, and stood.

Rodrigo Aguado met him at the office's threshold, wearing a broad grin as he thrust his hand toward Thatcher. They shook, and the Deputy Chief pumped his hand up and down with vigor. After the fifth pump, Thatcher disengaged with an uneasy smile.

"Please, Commander, have a seat." Aguado gestured at the sumptuous armchair that sat opposite his more modern-looking office chair.

Thatcher sank into the maroon pillow and stared over the desk as Aguado took his own seat.

He suppressed the urge to sigh.

"I don't mean to skip pleasantries, but I understand you're a busy man with places to be." The twinkle in Aguado's eye suggested he likely knew exactly what Thatcher was doing here.

The UNC probably knows everything that's spoken over an instant comm. They control them, after all.

Aguado put his hands on the desk, palms up, fingers curled slightly. "I understand you have information of some interest to the UNC."

"Yes."

"This is well. But before I request to know this information, I must know this thing first: what do you ask us in return?"

"Nothing."

"Nothing, Commander? This seems unlikely. You are not a

man to spread things across the Cluster for no reason. You're no gossip. For you to give us sensitive information—information whose sharing would likely upset multiple parties, if I have my guess—there must be a very good reason for this."

"I want the UNC to use the information I will provide to further its efforts to reopen a way back to Earth. I trust you'll do that regardless, so there's no need for me to request it outright."

Aguado's expression grew solemn, and he nodded. "You have family in Earth Local Space. A wife—Lin—and her parents. And your unborn child. You wish very much to return to them."

"Yes." Was Aguado worried Thatcher would change his mind about giving him the information? He didn't need his isolation from his family underscored. *Bureaucrats.*

"I understand. And my concerns, they are no more. Whatever information you have for me, you are giving it in good faith. What is this information, Commander?"

"You are aware of Frontier's recent mission to the Lacuna Region?"

"I am. You led this mission, correct?"

"I did." Thatcher sniffed. "You know, of course, that we encountered the Xanthic up there."

"I have seen video of your battle."

"Not all of it. Much of it was withheld. Especially the end, when their entire fleet disappeared through a wormhole of their own making."

Aguado steepled his fingers and leaned forward over the desk. His eyebrows twitched upward.

Initially, Rose had wanted to share the footage of the wormhole, as well as the fact that the Xanthic fleet they'd fought was almost certainly the same one that had attacked Earth Local Space fifty years ago. No one else seemed to have picked up on that, despite the footage being available for weeks. Was everyone so embroiled in war that they couldn't notice what was right in front of them?

Either way, Frontier's PR people had insisted against sharing those revelations, saying it would distract from Rose's efforts to defeat Daybreak. That was likely true, but by following the advice, wasn't she behaving in exactly the same way that had so frustrated her and Thatcher when it had come for others? She was effectively ignoring the looming threat while engaging in a war meant to further her own agenda. No matter how noble that agenda may or may not be.

Thatcher couldn't condone it. Nor could he remain silent.

"I'll give you footage of the wormhole opening and closing. As well as everything we copied from the Xanthic terminal we found, deep underground, in their colony on Recept." Thatcher drew a deep breath. "They have nanofab tech."

Aguado's eyebrows ratcheted higher. "Meaning Frontier now has it, as well?"

Thatcher met the Deputy Chief's eyes and said nothing.

The man's tongue probed the side of his cheek, causing it to swell out, and his eyes took on a distant cast. "I hope you understand we cannot sit on this information and do nothing, Commander. We will have to contend with the fact that Veronica Rose now has the ability to build nanofabbers. Which may lead to her uncovering you as the leaker of this information."

"I intend to tell her that myself." *Just not yet.* The knowledge could force her to recall him from the mission, before it had barely begun. As much as Thatcher hated to contemplate it, Frontier needed Moll. So he would secure the man's aid, and then tell Rose what he'd done.

"I see. You're doing the right thing, Commander. You know that, I'm sure."

Thatcher gave a curt nod. *Though I doubt Rose would agree.* He rose, and Aguado stood with him.

"I'll send you the information the moment I'm aboard my ship."

"Thank you, Commander. One last thing, however. Has it struck you as odd that Ms. Rose's techs were able to operate the Xanthic terminal's interface and navigate its operating system?"

"I…hadn't given it much thought." Thatcher frowned.

"The Xanthic technology we recovered from our first conflict with them has been kept highly classified ever since. Your techs have never before had the opportunity to study a Xanthic computer. Yet they cracked its security in quite a short span of time. Wouldn't you have expected the Xanthic technology to be a little more…alien?"

Thatcher narrowed his eyes. "Have you ever accessed a Xanthic computer?"

"I have not. Even my security clearance does not reach that high. I offer all of this as what you might call food for thought."

"I'll chew on it, then," Thatcher said slowly.

As they shook hands once more across the desk, Thatcher remembered sitting in Rear Admiral Faulkner's office, at the Hampton Roads Naval base. The admiral had been the one to order him to come here, and to accept Frontier's employment offer.

But his true mission hadn't been to serve Veronica Rose's interests. It had been to do his best to help unite the Dawn Cluster, and ready it to help humanity defeat the Xanthic.

So that was what he was going to do. For humanity. For his country.

And most of all, for Lin.

CHAPTER 14

Aboard the *Triumph*
Scanderoon System, The Splay
Earth Year 2290

Always keep your enemy on his back foot. Always keep him guessing.

The twelve Daybreak warships trailing Wilson's thirty-strong force across Scanderoon System certainly had to be guessing right about now.

"Scanderoon" was another word for homing pigeon, according to his eyepiece. *I suppose that's somewhat fitting.*

Once again, he'd infiltrated Daybreak space, and Herwin Dirk was going to be pissed off when he found out about it. This time around, they'd attracted a certain degree of attention.

Difficult not to, when you bring thirty ships with you.

The force trailing them had grown larger with each system they'd passed through. Enemy sensors couldn't help but pick up a fleet the size of the one Wilson now commanded, and it had clearly given enemy captains a lot to think about. Their own haphazardly assembled battle group consisted of too many damage dealers and not enough logistics ships, but that was because their force was made up of whatever ships had happened to be in the three Splay systems Wilson had taken his fleet through.

Aside from the enemy's composition, their battle group was also too small to engage the intruding Frontier fleet. And so they followed it instead, watching to see what Wilson would do.

They won't have to wait for long.

"Execute the course change," he ordered, speaking over the fleet-wide channel. "Now."

As one, the Frontier fleet fired lateral thrusters, causing each stern to swing twenty degrees to the right.

"Accelerate to maximum fleet velocity toward our target," he said. 'Maximum fleet velocity' happened to be as fast as the *Triumph* herself could sail.

The destroyer lurched forward, and a moment later the inertial compensators kicked in, Wilson's body swaying slightly forward in the process. He planted an elbow on one of the command seat's armrest, using a thumb to prop up his chin while his fingers played absently over his mustache. He studied his holoscreen.

Twenty-eight more Daybreak warships awaited them, arrayed around the Whitherward Trading Station. That force's composition was much more balanced than the one currently chasing them from the jump zone out of Agersia System. The larger force had plenty of damage dealers—destroyers, cruisers, corvettes, and frigates—and it also had the logistics ships to support them, as well as four eWar ships.

But to Wilson, even the larger force looked like a loose collection of ships rather than a cohesive unit. Then again, his formation had a similar appearance. That was by design. Had Daybreak also intentionally arranged its ships to give the appearance of disorganization?

Time will tell.

He cast his gaze around the *Triumph*'s CIC. His officers tapped smartly at their consoles. Each of them leaned forward slightly over his or her station, looking eager.

It seemed today's engagement would find them much less grim than they'd been during the last one. They were gradually embracing the rhythms of war. None of them enjoyed it, per se—at least, if they did, no one admitted to it. But Wilson had witnessed this many times before. The determination to protect. The righteous drive to avenge. Even the eagerness.

Part of their improved mood could no doubt be explained by the fact that today, they wouldn't be destroying any civilian installations. Whitherward's construction had been a joint project involving multiple corps, and destroying it wouldn't earn them points with anyone—Whitherward was far too important for commerce in the north. A massive station shaped like a child's spinning top, its girth rivaled some of the smaller nation-stations found in Sunrise System. It had a permanent population of thousands, mostly merchants and their families. Corps from all over the north brought their wares here, mostly to sell to each other.

No, Wilson wouldn't destroy Whitherward. Instead, he would take it.

He compared his force with the one arrayed around the station, and with the one giving chase across Scanderoon. All told, it would be his thirty ships against Daybreak's forty.

This will be the largest engagement the Cluster has ever seen.

The largest recorded engagement, at any rate. Though Wilson doubted there'd ever been a bigger one, recorded or not. If the secret skirmishes between corps had reached proportions like these, they wouldn't have been secret. And pirates couldn't muster forces this large. Not yet, anyway. Not even with the emergence of Degenerate Empire.

Kelly twisted in his chair to face the command seat. "We're five minutes from maximum firing range, sir."

"Acknowledged." Wilson tapped the new panel on his chair's arm, which put him on the fleet-wide channel. "The eWar squadron will slowly move to their designated positions in the second and third ranks. Logistics squadron, to the rear two ranks. Logistics, stand by to move forward and support whichever damage dealers receives the worst punishment from the enemy, and remember—do not raise shields unless you come under direct fire. We need your capacitors wholly devoted to keeping damage dealer shields up. To protect yourselves, take up positions directly behind whichever ship you're feeding power to."

As Wilson spoke, he'd punched in the ships his orders had been for. Now, indicators lit up green on his holoscreen, one by one, each one representing a ship that had heard and understood his orders. That was a new applet Veronica Rose's techies had designed for this purpose. Coordinating fleets this size represented an entirely new ball game, and Wilson felt glad to be fighting on the side that was figuring it out ahead of everyone else.

His fleet's two scout ships remained at the formation's rear, without needing to be told. They'd been brought primarily to range ahead during the journey through enemy territory, flitting into the next system before returning to transmit what they'd seen to Wilson. If this engagement required them to join the fight, with their limited weaponry, then it would be a bloody affair indeed.

The six logistics ships and five eWar ships finished moving into position just as they entered firing range. Enemy lasers flashed out across the battlespace, focusing on three separate targets—the *Triumph,* the *Snowbird,* and the *Lancer.*

Wilson took a moment to eyeball the enemy fleet before giving his next orders. It wasn't difficult to see Thatcher's handiwork in the way they'd arrayed themselves—the lessons he'd taught them by embarrassing them in battlespace after battlespace.

These were mostly top-of-the-line warships, not some loose collection of converted pirate scows. As a result, they all had shields, though it was impossible to tell how much capacitor power each vessel had to draw on in order to maintain them.

At any rate, each ship had raised their forcefields well before the Frontier ships had entered firing range, and they'd spread themselves out to increase their resistance to anything like Thatcher's Hellfire barrage.

But their target selection showed they were still a couple steps behind in the way they thought about space combat— which was exactly how Wilson liked it. They seemed to be hedging their bets, distributing their fire across targets that ranged from high- to medium-value.

You'll need to do better than that.

Another applet displayed the shield readout for each ship in Wilson's fleet, and it automatically shuffled those with the lowest shield power to the top. Wilson sniffed. "Logistics, focus microwave beams on *Snowbird* and *Lancer*, favoring *Lancer*." The cruiser was taking the most damage. As for his destroyer, she still had most of the capacitor modules he'd outfitted her with for the attack on Schesis, and she'd be able to hold out against the current barrage for some time.

That wasn't mere self-preservation, though Wilson admitted it did make him feel a little better. The main reason for keeping the additional charge capacity had to do with the fact the entire fleet, and hence the operation, would fall apart without its commander. They'd designated Captain Sooley of the *Lancer* to take over if Wilson fell, but in truth, he didn't trust anyone else to see this through. Except Thatcher, and he was dozens of light years away by now.

Wilson tapped smartly at his console. "All damage dealers focus primary lasers on the frigate I'm designating."

The target lit up red, both on his holoscreen and in the CIC's holotank, as it would in holotanks all across his fleet. He'd selected the frigate after noticing it had strayed a little too far from its own logistics ships for them to respond in time.

Sixteen beams of light slashed across the void, all converging on the slightly out-of-position frigate. Knocking down its shields and melting through its hull took just long enough for the enemy logistics squadron to respond, moving toward the afflicted frigate in an almost knee-jerk fashion.

You shouldn't have moved at all. The frigate exploded, and Wilson was already designating his next target, which the logistics ships' reaction had also left exposed.

"The corvette. Fry it."

'Fry it' hadn't been an order he'd been taught to give during his Prospective Commanding Officer course, but that had been a long time ago, and surely coming out of retirement to fight a war on the other side of the galaxy granted him *some* creative license.

Either way, the ships under his command seemed to understand the order. The lasers lanced out again. This time, one of the enemy logistics vessels got close enough to connect its microwave beam with the corvette's receiver array, but it added only twelve seconds or so to its existence.

The corvette ruptured, becoming a starburst of fiery debris slightly bigger than the frigate's had been.

This time, the opposing logistics squadron seemed to learn its lesson, dispersing itself more or less evenly throughout the fleet it was charged with supporting. What was more, the second Daybreak fleet was on the verge of entering maximum firing range on Wilson's ships, which would effectively sandwich him between two pissed-off fleets.

But he had no intention of letting that happen.

"All ships set a course through the enemy fleet, and prepare to engage that course at maximum acceleration. EWar, initiate omnidirectional jamming."

The applet indicating his orders had been understood began to light up green, before turning yellow across the board as friendly ships fell out of communication and vanished from sensors. At the same time, the *Triumph* lurched forward.

Flying blindly through an enemy fleet that was still twenty-six-strong couldn't be good for Wilson's blood pressure. The distances involved in space travel and combat were so vast that the chances of a collision were next to zero, but he still couldn't stop himself from imagining one all the same.

As the sensor fog cleared, the tactical display repopulated with the Frontier fleet now on the opposite side of the Daybreak force.

The next part would be the hardest. Wilson activated the fleet-wide channel once more. "All Nav and Helm officers will position their ships such that enemy ships of the first fleet are interposed between ours and the newly arrived fleet. *Now.*"

Using the enemy ships as shields would require minute calculations, as well as expert handling by his fleet's Helm officers. But Frontier only hired the best, and these officers were highly trained. He believed in them.

His logistics squadron continued to hide behind the ships they were servicing, saving on capacitor power by again side-stepping their own need for shields. That allowed them to maintain their charges' shields for even longer.

As for the enemy, their targeting was even sloppier than it had been before Wilson's order to jam their sensors. The range of the jamming hadn't been long enough to affect the second, smaller fleet, but that didn't seem to matter. The two enemy fleets were worse at coordinating with each other than the single one had been, and they tripped over each other, lacking a formation entirely, and for the most part unable to fire on the Frontier ships without hitting each other.

Wilson was using their superior numbers against them. And as the Daybreak vessels bumbled around the battlespace, he ordered his damage dealers to rip apart ship after ship.

After losing their eighth vessels without inflicting any losses at all on the Frontier fleet, the Daybreak forces had apparently had enough. They scattered in every direction.

Wilson ordered his force to break into packs—each comprised of two or three damage dealers, an eWar ship, and a logistics ship—which then chased down still more targets. They successfully neutralized a cruiser and a corvette before Daybreak managed to escape entirely.

With that, he recalled his ships to regroup around Whitherward Station, while a squadron of shuttles decoupled from the single Kibishii troop ship that had accompanied his force to Scanderoon System. They headed straight for the trading station.

Whitherward is ours. Now we just have to hold it.

CHAPTER 15

**Aboard the *New Jersey*
Enchiridion System, Sunlit Mesa Region
Earth Year 2290**

CARVING FORK IN ONE HAND, CARVING KNIFE IN THE OTHER, Thatcher attacked the Christmas turkey methodically, slicing a healthy portion for each officer and depositing it on his or her plate with a smile.

It was the fifth turkey he'd carved today. The biggest three birds had been for the mess deck, and the next-biggest for the chiefs' mess. The smallest—but still fairly sizable—turkey would be enjoyed in the wardroom.

His XO had selected large, healthy turkeys, and Chief Scott had outdone himself in their preparation. The meat was tender, and it looked succulent. Throughout the carving Thatcher had to swallow frequently to control his salivating. He would eat when the last officer had been served.

At Thatcher's orders, Billy Candle had procured the turkeys in Nova City, the capital of Bimaria. He'd also bought three artificial Christmas trees, and decorations—all during Thatcher's visit to the UNC headquarters.

The crew seemed surprised by the gesture, and even more by the fact that Thatcher was carving the turkeys himself.

By the time Thatcher finished carving and doling out servings, the turkey had stopped steaming, but it was still fairly warm. He cut himself off a large slice from the breast, then made his way to the buffet trolley, where dressing, cranberry sauce, slices of ham, and a bean casserole awaited him.

It took a considerable amount of willpower not to pile up his plate with a mound of food. Doing so would make him sleepy, and wouldn't have set a good example for his officers. But after staring at delicious food all day without being able to put any of it in his mouth, all he wanted to do was eat himself into oblivion.

Oh. He paused before leaving the trolley. He'd almost forgotten the gravy.

No need to be shy with the gravy.

He covered everything on his plate with the stuff.

As he took his seat, Tim Ortega walked over holding a beer can and grinning. "Don't forget your libation, sir."

Thatcher accepted the can, cracked open the tab, and saluted his chief tactical officer with it. "Cheers, Tim."

It was difficult to sip the beer through his wide grin, but he was altogether too pleased with himself for having Candle pick up the beverages along with the turkey and Christmas trees.

The beer was non-alcoholic. He'd successfully turned the *New Jersey* into a dry vessel. On Christmas Day. And the crew was *happy* about it.

Well, maybe not happy about *that,* specifically. But morale was high. And they would perform all the better for it. No spacer wanted to admit it, but alcohol impaired their effectiveness. Hangovers certainly did, but even alcohol consumed sometime in the last forty-eight hours made them more sluggish, whether they realized it or not.

Now, his vessel would be free from that particular affliction, just as U.S. Space Fleet ships were.

He was still grinning as he neatly separated his first bite of gravy-smeared turkey and lifted it to his mouth.

His comm beeped loudly and rapidly from its holster.

Everyone in the wardroom stopped eating and looked at Thatcher. They knew what it meant when a comm beeped that harshly. It was a priority transmission.

Thatcher lowered the fork to his plate and slipped the comm from its holder. He brought it to his ear. "Thatcher."

His XO spoke loudly through the speaker. "Sir, your presence is requested in the CIC, as soon as possible."

The officers in the wardroom sat perfectly still, waiting to see what Thatcher's reaction would be.

A captain's duty never ends. To show any sign of displeasure whatsoever at being called away from his Christmas meal before he'd even begun to eat it would do nothing for his crew's opinion of him. On the other hand, accepting the situation stoically would further cement his reputation of unflappability.

And that is the foundation of how a tight ship is run.

"I'll be there at once, XO."

He could see the glimmers of sympathy and admiration in his officers' eyes as he rose to leave.

"Ladies and gentlemen, I must leave you. Please have an extra helping in my stead." He smiled greatheartedly and made his way out of the wardroom.

This is an opportunity, really, he told himself as he strode briskly in the direction of the CIC, *to bind the crew even closer to me.* He tried to ignore the rumbling pit that was his stomach. *Everything is an opportunity.*

"It's a Russian battle group, sir," Candle told him as he settled into the command seat, battling with the irritation that threatened to commandeer his thoughts. "They appear to be following an intercept course with the *Jersey.*"

"Russian?" Thatcher said. "Ships from the Russian Space Navy were in the Dawn Cluster when the wormhole collapsed?"

"Uh, no, sir. I spoke imprecisely. We're looking at eight warships from a Russian private military company, Red Sky."

"I see." Thatcher turned his attention to his holoscreen, where he brought up a tactical display.

A destroyer, three corvettes, two cruisers, a frigate, and a logistics ship were moving to head off the *New Jersey*. That was simply far too many for the *Jersey* to fight, no matter what novel tactics Thatcher might come up with. Two freighters trailed behind the battle group, keeping their distance.

It was no secret that the *Jersey* was owned by Frontier Security, a corp that wore its American character proudly on its sleeve. Thatcher didn't know how the long-standing tension between his country and Russia would play out between their corporate proxies in the wake of the wormhole's collapse, and he wasn't keen to find out today.

Luckily, Sunlit Mesa was a cold region, where conflict between corps was virtually non-existent thanks to the heavy UNC presence. Indeed, there were two super-ships here in Enchiridion: a dreadnought and a drone carrier, keeping a watchful eye over the traffic passing through. Only the suicidally reckless would start trouble in front of two super-ships. The Russians were known for their brashness, but they had to know that if they broke the peace here, they'd never make it out of the system. Except maybe in one of the super-ship's brigs…if they were lucky.

Still, there was never any call to take unnecessary chances. "Candle, raise shields two minutes before we enter those ships' maximum firing range." Before Thatcher's arrival, Candle had been pulling double duty, having the conn as well as Tactical responsibilities. That had been acceptable in a cold system on Christmas Day—when there hadn't been a Russian battle group bearing down on them. Now that there was one, Candle was right to have called Thatcher here. "I also want firing solutions for the frigate and the corvettes, continuously updated as their positions change. If necessary, work with Nav to share the math work. Just get me that targeting data in time."

"Aye, sir."

Thatcher settled back in his seat and kept a close eye on the approaching battle group's posture. In the event they proved hostile, he could likely bloody their nose and rely on his shields to get him past their formation, bring his engines up to maximum acceleration, and take advantage of the Russians' momentum in the opposite direction in order to outstrip them. That would put him close enough to the UNC dreadnought for it to protect the *Jersey*, should the Russians prove insane enough to come after him.

The Red Sky battle group commander didn't attempt to contact the *New Jersey* until they were close enough for real-time radio conversation, which put them uncomfortably close to a range that would allow them to exchange blows.

"Captain Tad Thatcher, I presume?" The man in the holotank had brown, bushy dashes for eyebrows, overshadowing a serious face with piercing gray eyes. He spoke with a thick accent.

"That's right. Merry Christmas." The last two words came out as something close to a grumble.

"And you. I am Mikhail Volkov, CEO of Red Sky." Someone off-camera spoke to Volkov, causing him to frown fiercely at whoever was speaking. His gaze flitted past the camera, and he narrowed his eyes slightly before fixing them on Thatcher once more. "I see that you have raised your shields. Please allow me to put you at ease. We do not mean you violence this day."

"Then halt your ships outside firing range."

Volkov nodded sternly at one of his officers. Seconds later, Thatcher's Ops officer confirmed that the Russian ships had stopped.

"Helm, bring us to a halt as well."

The Russian captain spread his hands. "Perhaps now we can have a conversation."

"Go ahead."

"I come to you demanding an explanation."

"For what?"

"You work for Frontier Security, a key ally of Sunder Incorporated, and so when my sensor operator spotted your ship on radar, it seemed a perfect opportunity to get an explanation for what the hell Simon Moll thinks he is doing."

Thatcher slowly shook his head. "We're not sure where we stand with Sunder ourselves, actually. I'll remind you, Moll is also officially allied with the Daybreak Combine, with which Frontier is currently at war. Moll has taken no public position on that situation. In fact, we have no idea what he's doing. That's why I'm here—to find him, and to pin him to a position on the subject."

"I'll tell you what he's doing." Volkov's eyes burned even more intensely than before, which suggested he might not buy Thatcher's attempt to distance Frontier from Moll. "He's capitalizing on the unrest in the south to grab territory with both hands. Red Sky was ousted from Gabbro System for refusing to pay Sunder protection money."

"Gabbro. That's in The Brush." *What are Sunder forces doing that far south?*

"It's where our HQ is located. *Was* located. Look at the scorch marks near my frigate's nose. That was Sunder work—to show us they were serious."

Thatcher brought up a close-in visual of the Red Sky frigate. His eyes widened.

Volkov continued. "Moll forced us to abandon our facilities, load everything we could aboard our ships—hiring two freighters in the process—and flee. And that was just what we had in-system. We have assets spread across Lament, The Brush, and Fulmin, and no real way to coordinate them without an HQ for them to report back to. We have not yet been trusted with instant comms, as your American corporation has."

"If your assets are scattered across the southwest, then what are you doing in Sunlit Mesa?"

Volkov sniffed sharply. "We have come to request an instant comm unit from the UNC. At least, with that, we might be able to pay those on the network to relay a message to any Red Sky ships they encounter."

"I'm sorry I can't be of more help, Captain Volkov. But I can tell you that once I find Moll, I'll demand an explanation for the behavior you've described." *Among other things.* "If you're successful in obtaining an instant comm unit, feel free to contact me. I'll have my Ops officer transmit my contact ID to you now."

The Russian captain returned Thatcher's gaze with a glint of hunger in his eyes, as though he'd rather force Thatcher to hand over *his* instant comm unit, at the end of a primary laser.

Thatcher stared back, narrowing his own eyes slightly.

Finally, Volkov nodded curtly. "Very well. I will await your explanation with eagerness, Commander Thatcher. We have always had friendly relations with Sunder Incorporated. They have never behaved in this way before."

Maybe not. Thatcher drummed his fingers on his armrest once. *But I have a feeling they will again.*

CHAPTER 16

Aboard the *Triumph*
Agersia System, The Splay
Earth Year 2290

How did this fall apart so quickly? Wilson stared hard at the tactical display, willing his fleet to sail faster across Agersia System in its attempt to escape The Splay. *We were making such progress.*

"Daybreak forces are emerging into the jump zone out of Scanderoon, sir." Pete Kelly sounded strained as he made his report. "They aren't wasting time on sticking around to form up with the rest of the force as it comes through…the ships already in-system are headed straight for us."

Wilson narrowed his eyes at the news. "Acknowledged, Lieutenant." He didn't like how brazenly the Daybreak forces were stringing their ships across Agersia in their pursuit of the Frontier fleet. They had to know how badly Thatcher had punished enemies for doing exactly that.

It suggested a pack of ravening wolves chasing prey, who

know there are enough of their brethren in the area that they can afford to abandon caution.

Almost on cue, Kelly's body went rigid at the Ops station, and he turned slowly to face his captain. "Sir, more Daybreak forces are appearing out of Hyoid."

Wilson cursed, and the Ops officer winced slightly. "We have to take another way out," Wilson barked. "Nav, set a new course for the Agersia-Disomus jump gate, and engage it immediately. We'll have to take the same route out of The Splay that we took to enter it, when we attacked the mineral refinery in Schesis."

Will the corps in Laniferous System lift a finger against Daybreak, to prevent them from killing Frontier crews? Wilson wasn't willing to stake his life on it. Yes, the Laniferous corps had let Frontier warships pass through without hindering them or alerting Daybreak. But he suspected they would cower when confronted by the actual presence of their new masters.

He resisted the urge to slam a fist down on his chair's armrest.

Over the last weeks, Frontier strike forces had disrupted Daybreak supply lines, and attacked key targets distributed through The Splay's eastern systems, taking them or destroying them as optics demanded.

But their piecemeal push westward had been disrupted, and then reversed, in a matter of hours.

At least, Wilson was willing to bet that what had befallen his forces at Whitherward Station had also happened to the other Frontier forces in the region. An overwhelming number of allied Daybreak ships had poured out of two jump zones and converged on Wilson's fleet at Whitherward. No amount of clever tactics or superior coordination could have seen Wilson to victory. Not against a force that outnumbered his own almost threefold.

He'd held strong for a time, sending scout ships in two directions, toward systems where he knew Frontier battle groups had been dug in.

He'd meant to request their aid. But the scouts never returned, and he finally had to accept that Daybreak was going to regain Whitherward Station.

His delay cost Frontier five ships—*Eagleview*, *Pierre*, *Sojourner*, *Andrew*, and *New York*. Two frigates, an eWar ship, a corvette, and a cruiser. All gone, along with the good people who had crewed them.

The scale of the loss staggered him. He simply wasn't able to process it, beyond the fact that merely contemplating it made his stomach roil.

Days ago, the idea of commanding one side of the largest engagement in Dawn Cluster history had excited him. Now, he realized he'd broken another record. Humans had never fought other humans in space on this scale, ever. Nearly every lost ship represented hundreds of lives snuffed out, often in the space of a heartbeat. Only the *Eagleview* had managed to evacuate a significant portion of her crew, and Frontier ships had only been able to collect around half of those. They'd been forced to abandon the rest to the enemy.

If they're lucky, they'll be prisoners of war. If not, Daybreak will simply leave them to suffocate once they run out of oxygen.

Could Dirk bring himself to be that barbaric? Wilson prayed not.

Now, his forces fled through The Splay for their lives—and the lives of those left in Dupliss, defending military assets and civilian colonies. Before today, Wilson had known intellectually that the Cluster's hot zones had become lawless places, and that wrong moves could exact immense costs. But today, he was learning those lessons viscerally. They were slapping him full across the face, repeatedly.

If the Frontier forces couldn't consolidate and fight back in an organized fashion, how many would die? Did Dirk plan merely to oust Frontier from The Splay, or would he push all the way into Dupliss?

In his heart, Wilson knew the answer. Dirk would take this all the way to Oasis, if he could. What baffled him was how quickly the man had spun up his war machine—far faster than anyone had expected, including Wilson. It had been no mean feat, having to coordinate so many corps, and get them working together on a common cause.

They were still a disorderly mob, of course, but one large enough to sweep Frontier from the map all the same. And Herwin Dirk had spurred that mob into motion. For that accomplishment, Wilson had to give the devil his due.

"Sir, the *Constellation* just appeared in the jump zone out of Disomus. She appears undamaged."

"Acknowledged." Wilson gave a small prayer of thanks. The *Constellation* had been one of the two scout ships he'd sent to request reinforcements for Whitherward Station. It was a relief to know at least one of them had survived.

Soon after emerging into Agersia, the scout ship halted its forward acceleration, as though frozen in its tracks by the sight of two Daybreak forces streaming across the system in pursuit of Wilson's fleet.

Several minutes later, Kelly looked up from his console again. "I've just received a report from the *Constellation*, sir."

"Let's hear it."

"One of our battle groups is sailing through Disomus System. They were pushed out of Schesis by another Daybreak fleet, but that one didn't give chase. Instead, it accelerated north under what appeared to be full power."

No doubt to attack another one of our positions. So he'd been right. This offensive by Daybreak extended up and down The Splay's east side. A tide that sought to push Frontier out.

Burkov turned from the Tactical station to face Wilson, one

arm across the back of his chair. "Captain, if I may, a suggestion."

"Go ahead."

"Why don't we send the *Constellation* back into Disomus and have our battle group rendezvous with us just outside the jump zone? We can surprise Daybreak with our bolstered numbers. Destroy their ships by ones and twos as they appear in-system."

Wilson pursed his lips in thought. It was just the sort of tactic he favored, on a normal day.

But today, it seemed foolhardy.

"It would likely work," he told Burkov. "But there's too much risk of Daybreak forces showing up out of Schesis, or another neighboring system. If we get sandwiched in enemy territory, we're done for. Maybe *we're* willing to take that risk, but the defenders and civilians in Dupliss need us, and they need us now. I won't gamble with their lives."

Burkov nodded, shrugging. "Just a thought."

The Russian feigned nonchalance, but Wilson could tell the man was disappointed.

Well, so am I. He detested wasting any tactical advantage a battlespace gave him over his enemy. But taking advantage of this one seemed irresponsible.

I hope I'm right.

In a few hours, it was more than possible he'd be kicking himself for giving up the opportunity to diminish Daybreak's numbers, even by a little.

We'll throw them back at the regional jump gate, he told himself.

He just wished he could believe it.

CHAPTER 17

Aboard the *Victorious*
Dendriform System, The Brush
Earth Year 2291

Moll's invitation to come aboard his destroyer to meet with him personally had been suspiciously courteous. "You've come all this way," he'd said. "The least I can do is receive you aboard my ship."

Thatcher frowned down the passageway that stretched before him. Moll's words had been uncharacteristically pleasant, especially considering he'd been speaking to Thatcher. In the past, their conversations had rarely ever attained the heights of cordial, let alone warm.

This was his first visit aboard the *Victorious*, which was one more than he'd ever expected to make. Usually, Moll tried to discount Thatcher's rank and influence with Frontier, and when he couldn't do that, he strove to discredit him. But receiving him privately, in his office…

Thatcher didn't trust it one inch.

The Sunder CEO had sent his XO to meet Thatcher at his shuttle's airlock—a blunt-faced woman named Becker, who held the same rank Thatcher did.

Becker was courteous enough, and treated him with a base level of respect, but he noticed something odd about her. A quality shared by every other crewmember they passed on their way to Moll's office. Something he couldn't quite put his finger on.

The way they walked. Their easy, confident mannerisms. Their knowing smiles. They saluted Becker as she passed, including Thatcher in those salutes, but he got the sense they didn't truly consider him their superior.

Moll has certainly been busy. For all intents and purposes, Sunder Incorporated already held Candor in the palm of its hand. Even before the wormhole's collapse, virtually that entire region had been Sunder clients, paying the corp for securing their operations. Now, with how treacherous the Cluster's hot regions had become, they would no doubt be willing to do whatever it took to retain that protection. Like making endless concessions to their protector, including granting the company mining rights to asteroids, moons, and planetesimals in the systems where they held sway.

During Thatcher's journey through Candor Region, where Moll was nowhere to be found, and then through The Brush, he'd slowly put together the puzzle of exactly what the man had set his sights on. Based on the rumors he heard from captains he'd made remote contact with en route, and chatter over the instant comms net, Sunder appeared to have worked out some sort of deal with PMCs in The Brush—principally with Dynasty, a Chinese corp and the largest operator in the region. With their help, Moll seemed well on his way to controlling this region, too.

Becker came to an abrupt halt. "We're here." She knocked lightly on the hatch she'd stopped beside, three times, and immediately after the third knock the hatch swung inward with a light hiss.

"Thank you," Thatcher said, eliciting a curt nod from the woman. Before he'd fully crossed the threshold, she was already striding briskly away.

Moll's desk was less a desk and more a fortress. It was a solid hardwood U-shape that wrapped around him and prevented him from being flanked.

The CEO stood from his padded, ivory-colored throne of an office chair and spread his hands. "Commander Thatcher. Welcome." Moll gestured at the decidedly less throne-like chair opposite him. "Have a seat. Can I offer you a beverage? Non-alcoholic, I presume?" His mouth quirked upward at the corner.

Despite Moll's veneer of hospitality, Thatcher couldn't help but speak his mind. It wasn't in him to withhold things for the purpose of social lubrication. Or to play politics.

He remained standing. "When did you turn imperialist?"

"Please, Commander. Don't be so dramatic. Sunder is offering a service to the corps headquartered in The Brush. Nothing more."

"That's not what the CEO of Red Sky told me."

Moll showed no hint of surprise. Thatcher had to admit, the man had incredible self-control.

He settled into his ivory throne, scooted in to the mammoth desk, and folded his hands atop it. "Ah, you ran into Mikhail. How is he?"

"Not well, considering that his was one of the corps head-quartered here, and that you exiled Red Sky for refusing to pay you under your protection racket."

"It's not a protection racket if your clients actually need protection."

Thatcher barked a laugh. "Legitimate businesses don't normally drive prospective customers from their homes when they're not interested in the services offered."

At that, Moll frowned—the first crack in his magnanimous facade. "Red Sky was an instigator. A troublemaker. As you likely know, they occupied Gabbro, a system of great strategic importance, and refused to grant us access to it. Without it, we could not properly defend our other clients in The Brush."

Moll placed his hands on the desktop, palms down, studying their backs for a moment. He smiled up at Thatcher. This time, it was the cold smile of a predator. The mask of hospitality had fallen away. "I could have confiscated their assets and thrown their CEO in a holding cell to rot. It is within my power to do so, Commander. Who would stop me? But I am more civil than that, you see. So I allowed them to leave with everything they could carry."

Thatcher narrowed his eyes. "The fact you'd even bring up throwing an innocent man into captivity on a whim tells me—"

"Volkov is far from innocent. But that is utterly beside the point." Moll's smile fell away like a discarded carcass. "Veronica Rose needs a powerful ally, and she needs one immediately. Sunder Incorporated is willing to be that ally. But things have changed radically in the Dawn Cluster, Commander Thatcher, and I'm not convinced you fully grasp the implications yet. It is no longer enough to operate as a traditional Cluster private military firm, taking security contracts as they arise. We must be much more proactive than that. I agree with Ms. Rose that Daybreak Combine has proven morally unconscionable. But to meaningfully oppose a super-alliance of Daybreak's size, one needs a solid industrial power base. Sunder now has that base."

Thatcher felt his lips twitch. "So you'll help us bring Dirk to justice." That should have brought him relief, and it did, but not nearly so much as he would have expected. *I accomplished my mission. So why doesn't this feel like a victory?*

"Yes. However, this time, our alliance will be on my terms. Frontier will not seek to impose any conditions whatsoever on Sunder's operations. Neither should it expect any explanations or justifications for our actions. Frontier has proven exceptionally needy and demanding in the wake of the wormhole's collapse. I do not have time to suffer quibbling or equivocating any longer. I am too busy reshaping the Dawn Cluster."

Thatcher opened his mouth to speak, but Moll barreled on. "I will not take instruction from Veronica Rose, I won't take it from her pathetic weasel of a spymaster, and I certainly won't take it from you. You have my terms. I won't budge an inch on them. You may use the trip back to the *New Jersey* to consider them. After you arrive back at your command, I expect a prompt answer—yes or no. I assume Rose sent you with the authority to give it."

Thatcher met Moll's gaze steadily, grappling with an urge to leap over the U-shaped desk and throttle the man. "Very well," he said instead.

Moll's ingratiating smile returned suddenly, as though it had never left. "I believe our companies can have a very pleasant and fruitful relationship, Commander. So long as it is one built on respect."

I'm pretty sure I know which way Moll expects that 'respect' to flow. Without saying another word, Thatcher turned, opened the hatch, and left to make his way back to the shuttle, not bothering to wait for Moll to call Becker to guide him there.

Back on the *Jersey*, he told Candle everything while sitting in his own office, which was much smaller and less sumptuous than Moll's. He told him how unapologetic the Sunder CEO was about conquering The Brush in addition to Candor. And how the man apparently wasn't interested in concerning himself with the rights and freedoms of the civilians under his sway, since those were the only conditions Veronica Rose had ever sought to impose on Sunder. "I believe he's building an empire."

One of Candle's eyebrows shot upward. "Out of two regions?"

"That's one hundred and twenty-nine star systems, Bill. But I expect this is only the beginning."

"How much of the Cluster can he possibly expect to control? Where do you think his ambition caps out?"

Thatcher shook his head. "I'm not sure it does."

CHAPTER 18

Aboard the *Triumph*
Ecdemic System, Dupliss Region
Earth Year 2291

WELL, I CALLED IT. I'M NOW KICKING MYSELF.

Shortly after Wilson had failed to capitalize on the tactical advantage presented to him at the Agersia-Disomus jump zone, the order had arrived from Veronica Rose to keep Daybreak forces tied up in The Splay for as long as they could manage.

He'd thought the situation called for caution, but it turned out he'd simply failed to anticipate what his superior, Rose, would want. And she was right to want it. Freedom System would need as much time as it could get to prepare its defenses against the coming Daybreak onslaught.

Am I losing my touch? Or did I ever have it?

He'd already figured out that sitting in the command seat wasn't like riding a bicycle. After years away from it, his mojo hadn't come rushing immediately back.

But now he wondered if he might simply be the equivalent of

an outdated relic from another era, unsuited to this new scale and speed, as space combat matured and evolved.

He hadn't been too proud to learn from Thatcher, a much younger commander, who'd begun his career as a warship captain in this very environment. Wilson had taken notes from Thatcher's playbook, and some days he even liked to tell himself that he'd improved on the man's tactics.

But Thatcher was brilliant, whereas Wilson knew the best that could be said of him was that he was prudent and methodical. Great poets produced their best work in their early twenties, when their skills were still raw, their genius yet unshaped. He'd read that once. Space combat was a sort of poetry, and while Thatcher's twenties were behind him, perhaps a similar principle applied here.

Thatcher had "it." Did Wilson? He was beginning to worry that he didn't, any longer. If he ever did.

Suck it up, he told himself roughly. *You have a battle to wage, and a region to save. Dupliss needs a lot more than your self-pity.*

He really ought to give himself some credit, he knew. After Rose's order had arrived, he'd switched up his approach. He'd immediately started working to consolidate Frontier's forces and conduct hit-and-run tactics on the advancing Daybreak fleet.

The super-alliance had plenty of ships, but space was three-dimensional, and they could never cover all of it.

Wilson had his ships break from the ecliptic plane to get behind the enemy. They lay in ambush behind moons, crept through asteroid fields to thwart enemy sensors, and lurked in gas giants' vaporous atmospheres.

They'd managed to tie up Daybreak in The Splay for six days before finally being forced to flee through the regional jump gate back into Dupliss. They'd made mistakes, and they'd lost ships, but they'd destroyed more than they lost.

Six days. Was it enough? Could any length of time be enough?

Now, Wilson commanded the united Frontier attack force—some forty-nine ships, all told. It should have been fifty-four, but five more ships were unaccounted for, likely destroyed or captured.

Even so, it was the largest united force he'd ever been put in charge of, and a force set to engage in another record-breaking battle, just a couple of weeks after the record set by the engagement at Whitherward. This time, he didn't take an ounce of pleasure from that.

He'd arrayed his ships as close to the edge of the jump zone as he dared. Any closer, and he'd risk Daybreak damage dealers appearing close enough to surround Frontier ships and cut them off from the rest of his force.

I just wish we'd implemented everything Thatcher wanted. All the synergistic innovations the man had suggested…not just a comms channel that relayed the fleet commander's voice to every CIC, but every Nav officer on every ship working together, their consoles linked. Tactical too. Ops, and Helm.

It would improve everything. Speed of calculation, target selection, sensor data collection and interpretation, fleet organization and maneuvering, nimbleness, responsiveness…

But those protocols weren't in place yet, and the officers of his fleet weren't trained in them. So Wilson would just have to pull a miracle out of his ass some other way.

Pete Kelly's hands paused in midair over his console, and he brought them to rest on the ledge that ran along its bottom. "Sir, the first Daybreak ship has appeared. A scout ship. She's already trying to leave the jump zone for the jump gate back into The Splay."

Good luck with that. Wilson tapped the armrest panel and spoke over the command channel. "*Squall*, I want that target's sensors jammed."

The eWar ship's name lit up green on the command applet, signifying her captain had heard and understood the order to directionally jam the scout ship.

"The *Triumph* and *Minotaur* will hit it with lasers. Hose down those shields." The two destroyers bore plenty of capacitor modules, and they were among the ships he'd designated for burning down Daybreak shields as they entered the system.

Burkov gave a satisfied nod from his console, and the two destroyers lit up green on his applet. It wasn't much of an efficiency jump for Wilson to have his own CIC crew acknowledge his orders through the applet while he was speaking over the command channel, but it did help a little.

The enemy scout ship's shield wavered on the verge of collapse. "*Lancer* and *Nautilus*, finish her off. Three missiles apiece."

Four Hellborns and two Ogres streamed from the cruisers' missile tubes in quick succession. Some ships still carried the older ordnance, though the Ogres' onboard computers had been given a firmware upgrade to increase their resilience to hacking.

The first two missiles slammed into the scout ship, blowing her hull wide open. The second pair blew her to smithereens.

Figured that was overkill. Still, he'd rather risk overkill than failure.

I can't let their ships accumulate in the jump zone. I need to kill each one quickly.

After the scout ship's demise, the minutes piled up, along with the tension in Wilson's CIC.

The enemy's waiting for their scout to return. When it became clear it wouldn't return, the Daybreak fleet commander would know Wilson's forces were arrayed around the regional jump zone in the hopes of using the bottleneck it represented to nip the invasion in the bud.

Kelly went rigid at the Ops station. "Sir, a destroyer just appeared."

Wilson nodded. "They're going to try to muscle their way in." He tapped the armrest panel that switched him to the fleet-wide channel. "The *Triumph* and *Minotaur* will again hit with lasers, joined by—"

"Captain," Kelly said, drawing a sharp glance from Wilson. The Ops officer swallowed, then continued. "A frigate just jumped in. And—oh. A corvette."

Wilson found himself leaning toward his holoscreen to study the three newcomers. "Lasers. All designated shield breakers, select a target and fire your primary at one of those ships."

There wasn't time to designate ships to fire at specific targets. If his fleet's Ops and Tactical consoles had been linked, they could have selected their targets intelligently as well as rapidly. But under these circumstances, they could only do the latter.

As such, the destroyer ended up drawing way too much laserfire. "I want a few ships to redirect fire at the frigate and corvette."

The moment he spoke the order, Wilson realized his mistake. But it was too late: now, too few ships were firing at the destroyer, and its shields were stabilizing.

Damn it. I need to order the ships to retarget individually. Except, he wouldn't have time for that, once more Daybreak ships started arriving.

They managed to take down the destroyer and the frigate, but the corvette was still operational when the next Daybreak ship arrived in-system—another destroyer. A light-armored cruiser arrived hot on the heels of that, and then an eWar ship, followed by a logistics ship, a destroyer, and another logistics ship.

The Daybreak fleet commander's strategy took shape before Wilson's very eyes. He was sending in his sturdiest vessels, backed up by logistics ships to bolster their shields in order to get a foothold in Ecdemic while still more warships jumped to the system.

Then, something happened that Wilson should have predicted. The Daybreak eWar ship initiated omnidirectional jamming.

The Frontier fleet was too spread out for all its ships to be affected, Wilson knew, but the *Triumph* was one of those whose sensors and comms were washed out with noise.

It took several deep breaths to maintain his composure. *I should have seen this coming!*

As the command ship, the *Triumph* should have been positioned at the rear of the formation, where it would have been free from jamming. But now, he was cut off from distributing orders to the rest of the fleet, for as long as it took for countermeasures to clear the comms.

"Helm, full reverse," he barked. "Back us out of this sensor fog, now."

He felt himself drift forward against his seat's restraints, then the inertial compensators kicked in.

Hopefully, the Frontier ships not affected would have the presence of mind to single out the eWar ship with their lasers. But even that would no doubt take time, while Wilson's suddenly leaderless fleet struggled to reorient itself. No one could blame them for experiencing confusion at suddenly losing contact with their leader.

I've completely failed to account for the realities of fleet combat at this scale.

"Sensors are clearing, sir. Sir...." Pete Kelly twisted in his seat to face Wilson, his mouth working but producing no sound.

Wilson looked at the tactical display shown in the CIC's holotank, and his heart rate spiked.

Fifteen new ships had appeared in Ecdemic while the *Triumph* had been finding its way out of the sensor fog. As he watched, a frigate appeared, followed immediately by a cruiser.

Clearly, Daybreak was sending their ships through the jump gate stem to stern, at a rate that didn't seem altogether safe.

But it was effective. The jump zone was filling up with enemy ships.

From the *Triumph*'s removed vantage point, where Wilson could oversee the engagement and give out orders free of jamming, he coordinated his damage dealers as effectively as he could. They still outnumbered the in-system Daybreak forces by over two-to-one.

An enemy destroyer went down, followed by a corvette, and then a frigate. But the Daybreak attack force was regrouping, and returning fire, though their targeting wasn't nearly as efficiently as the Frontier ships'.

The enemy lost roughly two and a half ships for every Frontier vessel they destroyed, but it still wasn't enough.

Wilson couldn't stomach the losses any longer. It wasn't just the fact that Daybreak had the numbers to lose ships at this rate and still win. It was also the experience of watching each Frontier ship get destroyed, and the knowledge of how many families had just lost loved ones.

How many mothers had lost sons.

How many wives, their husbands.

How many brothers, their sisters.

"Disengage," he said, but the word came out hoarse and low. He cleared his throat. "Disengage. Destroyers, cover our smaller ships' retreat. EWar, prepare to engage omnidirectional jamming."

We'll fall back to the next system, and we'll use that jump zone as the bottleneck. We'll do it better, this time.

But even disengaging had its own costs, and more Frontier ships fell even as they fled for their lives.

CHAPTER 19

Aboard the *Triumph*
Freedom System, Dupliss Region
Earth Year 2291

TEN DAYS. HE'D STALLED THE ENEMY'S ADVANCE FOR TEN DAYS before being forced back into Freedom System.

The same thought repeated in Wilson's head as he watched Daybreak ships pouring into the jump zones out of Carillon and Mislit:

They have us right where they want us.

We should have been able to stall them for longer. He'd tried to use each jump zone as a bottle neck to bag more targets, but the enemy fleet commander had been smarter than that. Now that he'd infiltrated Dupliss, he had the luxury of sending a flanking force through other systems, to sandwich the waiting Frontier forces at each jump zone.

Wilson's scouts had spotted the flanking force coming each time, and he'd ordered a retreat to the next system—surprising the second force by engaging it whenever a system's jump gate distribution allowed him to quickly withdraw if needed.

Mostly, though, he'd fallen back endlessly, and bought Frontier little more than a week.

After his force was thrown back into Freedom System, he'd expected Dirk to send his ships flooding in after them immediately. Instead, he'd made them wait—for four more excruciating days.

The waiting had been worse than the engagements. Even defeat after defeat had been preferable to the dreadful anticipation of Frontier Security's ultimate demise, which could begin at any moment.

Why do they hesitate? he'd wondered, more than once.

Then the reports had come in of a second Daybreak fleet, moving south through Dupliss from the Kreng Region. That journey must have taken longer than Dirk had anticipated, since the force was clearly sent in hopes of catching Frontier ships out in the field, cutting them off from Freedom, and completely surrounding them.

But that hadn't happened, and the Daybreak commander, whoever he was—so far, Wilson had seen no sign that Dirk himself was with the attacking force—had apparently decided to wait until their entire invasion force was united.

The delay had brought two unexpected upsides, but Wilson was far from convinced they would be enough.

One, it had given him time to prepare the system's defense exactly how he wanted it.

Two, it had allowed Thatcher and Moll to get within seven hours' travel time of Freedom System. The *New Jersey* sailed at the head of a twenty-five strong Sunder fleet. Wilson would have liked more, but according to Thatcher almost half of the Sunder warships were destroyers. It had probably been word of Thatcher's approach that had spurred the enemy fleet commander into action.

But it didn't matter. Thatcher was too late. In the hours it would take for him to get here, Frontier Security could be wiped from the star charts.

Every company ship had returned to Freedom, recalled from the various corners of the Dupliss Region where they'd been stationed. All of Frontier Security had assembled, along with a battle group's worth of Kibishii troop ships.

It wasn't enough. Not nearly.

I have tricks up my sleeve yet, he told himself. But even knowing the surprises he had in store for Dirk, or for whoever he'd appointed as his fleet commander…it didn't bring Wilson much comfort. One of those surprises constituted something he never would have expected Frontier to find itself resorting to. It would set a dark and dangerous precedent for the Dawn Cluster.

The Kibishii ships were all lying in wait behind the jump zone out of Mislit System, in stealth mode. Wilson had ordered them out there, to remain hidden until an optimal number of Daybreak ships had collected within the jump zone, preferably clumped together.

When the moment arrived, the Japanese warships would open fire using the missile tube modules they'd installed at the Helio bases that orbited Oasis.

Wilson frowned across the CIC, at the holotank, which showed Daybreak's forces loitering near both jump zones. He'd dared to hope that the enemy commander would be inexperienced enough to let his ships stream across the system in a staggered line, but no such luck. Clearly, they were waiting to advance together.

Do they plan to wait until their entire force is assembled? If they did that, Kibishii would likely never get the chance to fire on the enemy from hiding. Engaging too many enemies at once would risk losing all of their ships.

Out of nowhere, it occurred to Wilson that he occupied the exact same position that Reardon Interstellar's Ramon Pegg had once been in, when Tad Thatcher and Simon Moll had led a force against his entrenched position around Oasis.

He didn't like that feeling one bit.

"Sir," Pete Kelly said, the rest of whatever he'd been about to say choked off as he sputtered for words.

Wilson's eyes snapped back to the holotank, to the part that represented the jump zone out of Mislit. There, a fleet's worth of Daybreak ships had broken off from their fellows and were firing lasers on the hidden Kibishii ships.

Except, clearly they aren't hidden, are they?

The Kibishii captains hadn't had shields raised, since the energy signatures would have blown their cover. But their cover had been blown all along. One of the troop ships burst apart under the focused fire of Daybreak beams, and the enemy smoothly switched to the next target.

Forcefields flickered to life around the Japanese warships, and they began to accelerate backward under full power. As they did, another ship exploded from the energy being dumped into her.

How were they able to foil Kibishii's stealth tech?

Pete Kelly spoke up, apparently having found his voice. "Captain...Meridian is heavily represented among the ships attacking the Kibishii vessels."

Meridian. The corp that had attacked Kibishii for months, all while denying it. Their behavior had played a large part in starting this war.

So they've cracked the current generation of stealth. That can't mean good things.

As the Kibishii troop ships retreated toward deep space, the remainder of the Daybreak forces started across the system, charging toward Oasis from two separate jump zones. Behind them, a steady stream of additional ships continued to arrive from Carillon and Mislit.

CHAPTER 20

Aboard the *Triumph*
Freedom System, Dupliss Region
Earth Year 2291

DAYBREAK WARSHIPS CHARGED ACROSS THE SYSTEM, AND ALL was still inside of Wilson's CIC.

The only sounds were the *Triumph*'s usual humming and creaking, along with the occasional pop and hiss of coolant running through pipes behind the bulkheads.

The only motion was the rise and fall of his crew's shoulders as they all watched the holotank with rapt attention. In particular, their gazes were fixed on Cronus, the gas giant whose orbit had put it close to the route between Oasis and the Freedom-Carillon jump gate.

As the enemy forces drew level with the gaseous planet, Wilson focused on keeping his breathing steady, both hopeful and fearful for what would happen next.

There.

The sound of uniforms rustling could be heard throughout

the CIC as crewmembers leaned closer to the holotank, or turned to their own holoscreens to pull up tactical displays.

A yellow dot had emerged from the great orb representing Cronus. Another joined it, then another.

At first, the Daybreak ships showed no sign of reacting, either unsure what the blips represented or at a total loss for how to respond.

Then, as more and more yellow dots emerged, to form a dispersed cloud many thousands of kilometers in diameter, the advancing line of Daybreak ships bent away from it like a dam breaking.

They were missiles, emerging from the gas giant to chase after the enemy ships.

Wilson noticed his breathing had accelerated, and he closed his eyes, willing himself to calmness.

On the heels of the barrage, ten small, sturdy-looking vessels emerged, spitting more missiles as they went, adding to the volley.

They were called tropodivers, ships capable of surviving the extreme conditions found in a gas giant's troposphere, where winds reached six hundred and seventeen kilometers per hour.

The feat was the product of several new technologies, all of which were now available on what was effectively the Dawn Cluster's black market.

Of course, the UNC can't enforce any regulations, anymore. The black market is pretty much just the market.

The tropodivers' hulls couldn't withstand the bottom of Cronus' troposphere, where the pressure was the same as it was at Earth's surface. But they could still go pretty deep, which allowed them to cruise along inside the gaseous clouds, building up a Hellfire barrage that no sensor could detect. Pulling it off had required the invention of a new type of sensor, one capable of discerning direction via minute pressure differentials across several different sections of a ship's hull.

The tropodivers' missiles were also specially designed for the extreme conditions, with the ability to intelligently select targets once they emerged from the gaseous atmosphere. They came with a grim little name of their own: Eliminators.

Threatening enough.

The missile cloud divided itself up, devoting a number of Eliminators to each target calculated to overcome the firepower the enemy was likely to devote to shooting it down. For a few long minutes, it seemed that the Daybreak shields would absorb the ordnance.

Then, bright beams flashed from the tips of the frontmost missiles. The Eliminators carried laser warheads, and the first wave weakened the enemy forcefields before being shot down. The second wave softened those shields further, and by the time the third wave came into play, shields began to fall, making way for Eliminators to slam into exposed hulls.

The ten gas-diving spacecrafts belonged to a corp that had started up in the wake of the wormhole's collapse, and this was its first contract. The corp's like had never been seen, neither in the Cluster nor Earth Local Space. Called Celeste Security Solutions, they were a PMC that exclusively served PMCs. Celeste existed solely to help military corps wage war on other military corps.

Mercenaries, essentially.

Wilson had to hand it to Selene Williams, Celeste's CEO—she had a head for business. Celeste's services were designed to fill a defined and hungry niche: system defense, with a focus on helping smaller corps protect themselves against larger ones. The underdog factor would go a long way toward counteracting the stigma always attached to the term 'mercenary,' though it could also backfire by making Celeste a lot of powerful enemies.

Whether the mercenaries would hit their PR stride didn't particularly concern Wilson. Their existence, however, did.

It's dangerous. If this caught on—and Wilson felt pretty

confident it would catch on—then the Cluster would fill up with military corps who had no HQ, no ties to even a star system, let alone a nation.

A Daybreak destroyer went down first, followed seconds later by a frigate, and then an eWar ship. The missiles didn't discriminate between ship types, but simply went for the most viable targets. Next, a light armored cruiser ruptured, flinging flame and debris in every direction.

Wilson's heart leapt, then sunk again as his thoughts turned to what Frontier's use of Celeste Security Solutions would mean. For one, it would weaken Frontier in the eyes of the Cluster. How could they claim to be formidable when they relied on another PMC to defend its own system?

There were other reasons to worry about the rise of this sort of corp. Celeste didn't have American interests at heart, or the interests of any nation. It would fight for the highest bidder. Where did that leave humanity, especially when it came to achieving unity throughout the Cluster so they could fight the Xanthic together?

Thatcher talks about that a lot. But everyone else seems to have forgotten about it.

Unity had its dangers, too. What if the Cluster's corps did unify—or if one corporate alliance won out, becoming the dominant force and bending the others to their will? What if it grew large enough to challenge the UNC?

A lot of people disliked how powerful the UNC had become. But would a corporate overlord be preferable? One driven by bolstering its bottom line via any means necessary?

If one corp becomes dominant, it has to be Frontier. That was one of the main reasons Wilson had come out of retirement: to make sure it *was* Frontier.

In the end, Celeste's missile barrage destroyed thirty-two Daybreak warships. That number was equal to over a quarter of Frontier's entire remaining fleet.

And it's still not enough.

The massive barrage finally spent, Daybreak ships surged after the mercenaries, no doubt intent on chasing them down and taking their revenge by destroying them one by one.

But the Celeste captains had clearly expected that. Their ships were already fleeing in the opposite direction, toward the gas giant. They reached it well before their pursuers entered maximum firing range, disappearing unceremoniously beneath Cronus' orange-white clouds.

There wasn't much the Daybreak fleet commander could do about that. The super-alliance's ships were numerous, but they weren't built to dive as deep as a gas giant's troposphere. Even if they could, how would they navigate it?

So thirty-eight ships remained distributed across Cronus' roiling surface, no doubt positioned to disrupt a second barrage, and to destroy the Celeste ships in the process.

Wilson knew the second barrage would never come. The mercenaries had anticipated this move from Daybreak—during negotiations, they'd only agreed to a single attack.

Still, keeping almost forty more ships tied up is a help to us. Celeste's sneak attack had been a massive success. There were still far too many Daybreak ships in Freedom System, but maybe Frontier would have a chance, now. Of survival, if not victory.

Even after devoting ships to chasing Kibishii into deep space, losing more to Celeste's attack, and leaving thirty-eight to hold orbit over Cronus, Daybreak still had a fleet one hundred and eighty-seven strong to send at Oasis.

Frontier had only one hundred and five remaining warships to defend the planet. *And I have just one more trick up my sleeve.*

Lieutenant Kelly exhaled in an audible *whoosh.* "Sir, the enemy's foremost ships will enter maximum Hellborn range in five minutes."

"Acknowledged." Wilson tapped the panel on his chair's armrest to switch him over to the fleet-wide channel, patching his voice through to the CICs of over a hundred ships. "All vessels, begin transition to lower orbits."

Immediately, the rectangles on his command applet started lighting up green, as the ships under his command acknowledged the order by the dozen. The tactical display also reflected the order, as his entire fleet huddled a little closer to Oasis' surface.

He wanted the move to look like a reflexive, desperate one, and he expected it to be convincing. The fact that they were giving up the 'high ground,' so to speak, should help sell the idea. It was harder to fight a ship that occupied a higher orbit than you, since you had to shoot up against a gravity well to do it.

The fact that the move truly was born of desperation would probably also help with making it convincing.

The Daybreak fleet surged forward. Their captains would feel confident doing so, since they weren't even in range of the Helio bases' turrets yet. With their numbers, they would be able to disable each base's artillery with ease, and then proceed to rain destruction down on their foe.

Except, the Helio bases had more teeth than they seemed to expect.

As the Daybreak ships drew near, Hellborns launched from four newly installed hard points, where repair bays once had been. Wilson had made the recommendation to Veronica Rose weeks ago, and she'd given the order to carry it through.

The first missiles carried laser warheads, as was becoming standard practice. Beams lashed out from their tips, knocking down shields around the unsuspecting vessels.

This was another risky play, Wilson knew. It was the first time in Cluster history that a Helio base had been used so aggressively. Yes, in the cold regions they usually had turrets, but those were mostly for fending off pirates. The fact the bases were largely staffed by civilians meant no one expected them to play a significant role in large-scale conflicts.

But this was about survival. And Wilson meant to survive.

Seven Daybreak warships fell to the barrage, and two more took significant damage. Unfortunately, the losses were followed by another Cluster first.

The enemy ships focused their own missile volley on the Helio base. It took a mix of just eleven Ogres and Hellborns to compromise the superstructure, ripping it apart and exposing the base's innards to space.

In the shocked silence that followed, Wilson stared across the CIC at the holotank. The move hadn't been completely unexpected—they'd evacuated the base almost completely before the first Daybreak ship had entered the system.

It made sense to fire back at anything that fired at you.

Still, Helio bases formed the backbone of the Dawn Cluster's economy. And no matter how much tactical sense its destruction had made, Veronica Rose would undoubtedly spin it to make Daybreak Combine look like heartless savages.

There had been civilians still aboard that base. Frontier had evacuated all they could, but a few had refused to leave it, calling the base their home.

Wilson drew a deep breath to steady his voice, then put himself back onto the command channel. "All ships, make for the nearest intact Helio base. Gradually transition to a higher orbit as you go."

But the surprise missiles from the destroyed Helio base had barely broken Daybreak's stride, and they harried the Frontier ships all the way to the next orbital stations.

Wilson had to wonder if putting the bases at risk had been worth it. Even if it had destroyed seven more ships.

As his warships positioned themselves around the remaining Helio bases, and turned to confront their pursuers, the Daybreak captains didn't hesitate. Instead, they took advantage of the temporary confusion and targeted the bases first.

It cost them a total of eleven ships to do it, but first one base burst apart in a cascading explosion of flaming debris…and then, so did another.

"Fall back," Wilson said over the command channel, his voice coming out as a barely audible rasp. "Fall back to the other bases, and fire on the enemy ships as you disengage."

Before he'd finished speaking, the enemy switched their focus to the retreating ships, and three more Frontier vessels went down.

CHAPTER 21

New Houston, Oasis Colony
Freedom System, Dupliss Region
Earth Year 2291

As he walked into the Frontier Security board room, Thatcher felt like his veins were buzzing with the large coffee he'd just shotgunned.

Every step was like lifting a leaden weight. He felt light-headed—like his reality had taken on a thin, brittle aspect, one that could shatter at the slightest jolt.

During the past few weeks, he'd slept very little. Moving through the Dawn Cluster's cold regions as fast as the *New Jersey* was capable of moving without shuddering apart at the frames…well, it turned out that required a lot of attention from a ship's captain. From UNC ships demanding to know where he and the Sunder fleet were headed in such a rush, to transmissions as trivial as bottom feeders trying to sell them salvaged parts, probably pirated—it had all required a firm hand on the rudder to keep his ship sailing smoothly through space.

But they'd done it. They'd arrived before…

...before what?

He attempted to blink the bleariness away as he settled into one of the seats arranged around the board room table. Everyone else here looked about as haggard as he felt, so he shouldn't allow himself too much self-pity.

Yes, the *Jersey* had arrived with the Sunder warships in time to avoid Frontier Security's utter destruction. But the death toll from Daybreak Combine's attack was in the thousands, and the company had lost over half its total fleet.

Those present in the board room who'd participated in the battle looked haunted, their eyes staring into a distance only they could see. Wilson had acknowledged Thatcher with little more than a nod and a grunt, but he didn't take that personally.

The Kibishii CEO, Akio Hata, sat to the right of Veronica Rose's empty seat. Apparently he'd been on one of his troop ships when they'd been surprised by Daybreak's ability to see them, and his ship had taken significant damage to its bow, though its structural integrity had remained intact. His shoulders were hunched, and he stared solemnly at the tabletop, as though the oaken surface might hold the answer to a long-pondered riddle.

Even the board members looked shaken. Out of everyone in the room, only two men looked more or less composed: Simon Moll and Hans Mittelman.

They sat as far away from each other as possible, Moll at the end of the table opposite where Rose would sit, and Mittelman at Rose's left hand. The spymaster was pointedly avoiding the Sunder CEO's gaze, but Moll's smirk suggested that he barely noticed Mittelman's attention—or feigned lack of attention. Mittelman might as well have been a cockroach, for all Moll seemed affected by his presence.

What happened between those two? Thatcher hadn't heard of any conflict between them, but the way they were behaving toward each other spoke volumes.

Rose appeared at the double doors, which were propped open. She managed a faint smile, though she stumbled as she made her way around the table, and Thatcher winced. It seemed she'd been getting about as much sleep as he had, lately.

When she made it to her seat, she planted her hands on its back instead of sitting. "Welcome back, Commander Thatcher, and a thankful welcome to you, Simon. If Sunder hadn't agreed to accompany the *New Jersey* back to Freedom System, there would no longer be a Frontier Security. And so I offer you my sincerest thank you. We are in your debt."

Moll's smile widened, at that. And Thatcher's heart sank a little more.

But there was no use living in denial. *Rose is right.* Herwin Dirk had clearly wanted to finish Frontier. Even after the arrival of the *Jersey*, with a fleet of Sunder warships at its back, Daybreak had taken a long time to admit defeat. They'd fought almost to the last, and the prolonged fighting had exacted a heavy toll on both sides.

Sunder had lost six ships—three completely destroyed, and three disabled, their crews evacuated. That would count as a devastating loss on any day. But today, next to the Frontier and Kibishii losses, it seemed Moll had gotten off lucky.

A lot of Frontier crews *had* managed to evacuate their damaged ships, so there was that to be grateful for. But a significant number of them had been taken hostage aboard Daybreak shuttles, amidst the confusion of battle. And many crews had been lost altogether.

"Having said that," Rose continued, "there's something about Sunder's recent behavior that concerns me."

Moll's smirk remained in place, but his eyes grew cold and harsh. He turned his head toward Thatcher, and their eyes met. Thatcher held the man's gaze without flinching. He could almost hear the silent conversation they were having. What Moll was accusing him of with his eyes: *You told her about our activities in The Brush. Didn't you?*

And Thatcher, with his steadiness: *Of course I did.*

"It has come to my attention," Rose said, glancing between the two of them, "that Sunder has been conquering systems in the Dawn Cluster's south."

Moll barked laughter at that. "'*Conquering?*' You can dispense with the propaganda, Veronica. Your usual audience isn't privy to this meeting, so far as I know."

"Call it what you will. I have received complaints from multiple corps, who know that Frontier is closely allied with Sunder. They say you ousted them from their territory."

"I'm doing what's necessary to stop Herwin Dirk from taking over the entire Cluster. And would you please drop the self-right-eous act? You've already proven yourself willing to do whatever it takes to win, just as I have, so you shouldn't pretend to be as naive as your favorite commander here."

Rose's eyes flitted to Thatcher's face, then back to Moll's. She said nothing.

"Let's not forget who signed off on making Frontier the first company ever to deploy a mercenary corp in battle." Heedless of the glares his words attracted from around the table, Moll pressed on. "Or who made the decision to put Oasis' Helio bases in danger, losing four of the six, and sacrificing civilian lives in the process."

Moll swept the board room table with his gaze, sneering back into the resentful faces turned toward him. "I *saved* you. No dance of words can mask that fact, nor can any baseless accu-sations.

Rose shook her head. "No one is trying to—"

Moll talked over her. "As for Sunder's actions in The Brush, what we really did was offer a life-saving service to dozens of corporate clients, representing hundreds of thousands of employ-ees, along with the civilians they're charged with safeguarding.

The few who were forced to leave the region stood in the way of that life-saving service.

"You need an ally, Ms. Rose. Badly. Just as badly as you did during the thick of Daybreak's slaughter today. Because Herwin Dirk will not stop until Frontier is scrubbed from the star map." Moll tapped a thick finger on his chest. "I am willing to be that ally. Sunder Incorporated is willing to be that ally. But only if you're willing to accept us on terms that aren't patently insane. If you can bring yourself to do that, then together we can defeat Dirk."

Thatcher felt like he should say something. But what was there to say? That Moll only wanted to defeat Dirk so Sunder could take its territory?

He suspected that was true—especially judging by the growing number of mining, cargo, and construction ships that had joined them as they'd sailed through Candor Region. But saying it out loud would risk shattering their alliance with Sunder…which would likely mean Frontier's end. Thatcher had gone against Rose on principle many times before. Publicly. But even he couldn't oppose her in this.

Moll brought a fist down firmly onto the table. "We need to go on the offensive. Now, while Daybreak is weakened."

Akio Hata spoke up. "We, too, are weakened." Even the man's voice sounded weak.

"We won't be for long. I propose we strike deep into the heart of The Splay, to take Bakelite. It's a crossroads system, not just for The Splay but for Kreng and Endysis regions too. Plus, the twin mineral refineries it holds has become even more vital, since you destroyed the one in Schesis. If we can gain a foothold there—and I believe we can—then we can end this war."

A weighty silence ensued as every eye drifted to the end of the table, where Veronica Rose was finally taking her seat.

She met Moll's eye across the long board room table, and while she seemed just as self-possessed as ever, Thatcher couldn't help but think there was an air of defeat in the tired way her mouth curled downward at the edges.

"Very well. Captain Wilson, you will remain in Freedom, to coordinate our defense with Celeste Security Solutions. Commander Thatcher…the *New Jersey* will accompany Sunder on the mission to take Bakelite. So will a Frontier battle group, which you will command."

"Yes, ma'am," Thatcher said with a nod. He couldn't help feeling guilty about Rose's show of renewed trust in him, given the way he'd betrayed her to the UNC in Clime.

But he'd only done what he had to do.

As always.

CHAPTER 22

New Houston, Oasis Colony
Freedom System, Dupliss Region
Earth Year 2291

Thatcher woke to his comm's alarm app blaring in his ear.

He blinked up at the ceiling for a few seconds, then scooped up the comm from the bedside table.

His heart leapt into his throat.

Thirty minutes? He'd been sleeping through the wakeup alarm for thirty minutes.

In less than a second, he was on his feet and running for the washroom, the bedclothes tossed onto the chamber's floor in his haste.

He relieved himself, then scrubbed his teeth while trying to whip his foggy thoughts into shape. His shuttle for the *New Jersey* was due to leave in another thirty minutes. What did he need to do in order to be ready at the spaceport in time? And what could he afford to skip?

He looked down at his toothbrush. It didn't have any tooth-paste on it.

He'd forgotten to use toothpaste.

"Get a hold of yourself," he told his reflection sternly. With that, he squeezed the white gel onto the brush and scrubbed all the more vigorously at his teeth, which weren't as white as he would have liked.

Need to cut back on the coffee. And start using the baking soda and hydrogen peroxide again. Get them sparkling like elephant tusks.

He shook himself. Good Lord, he *was* in a different state of mind, wasn't he?

He was forced to skip his shower, opting instead for a quick wash with a cloth. Thankfully, his short brown hair didn't give him much trouble, other than a tuft near the back which refused to stay down until he'd tackled it with a wet comb at least ten times.

Luckily, his uniform had accumulated few wrinkles the previous day, and he'd hung it up before bed, as was his custom. There was no time to press it.

Fifteen minutes after waking to the obnoxious blaring of his alarm, he was dashing through the hallways of Frontier HQ, duffel bag swinging wildly at his side.

At the first intersection, a voice called from a crosswise corridor. "Captain."

He froze in his tracks, his stomach sinking. He'd recognized the voice instantly.

He turned to see Lucy Guerrero striding toward him, immaculate in her crisply pressed uniform. Her polished boots flashed in the halogens' light.

It was exactly the wrong time for this reunion. Besides which, he wasn't the slightest bit prepared for it.

"Lieutenant. Guerrero. Lucy." He forced himself to take a deep breath. "I'm afraid I can't talk. I have to go." With that, he broke into a full-on run, continuing in the direction he'd been going.

"Sir, I was hoping to speak with you while you were on Oasis." The patter of her boots told him she was running after him, and gaining rapidly. "Except, after that meeting you went straight to your chambers. I didn't want to disturb you."

"This isn't a good time," he said as Guerrero caught up, loping along beside him like a gazelle fresh from a winter's hibernation. *Do gazelles hibernate?* Thatcher glanced at Guerrero. *I guess she's been keeping up with her PT.*

"Sir, I'd like to be reinstated to active duty."

"What does Doctor Weber say?"

"She said it's up to you. She cleared, me but…"

He raised his eyebrows at her, trying not to pant. "But?" Guerrero still showed no sign of exertion.

"But she said I'm prone to relapse, if I don't manage my stress levels."

Thatcher tried to sort through his thoughts, which weren't nearly as muddled as they had been, although worrying whether he'd make his speeder to the spaceport on time *was* occupying plenty of mental space. Not to mention continuing to run with a duffel bag while trying to have this conversation. He switched the bag to his left hand.

When he finally spoke, the words came out sounding somewhat breathy. "I know I've been an…exacting commander. Lately, I'm trying not to be *quite* so exacting. While still maintaining the standards I consider necessary to maximize effectiveness," he added quickly.

Guerrero nodded.

"Even so, the job itself is stressful enough all on its own. And Lucy, I can't guarantee stress levels won't exceed the level you're capable of tolerating."

They turned a corner, the duffel bag swaying outward and jerking his arm in the process. They'd arrived at the elevators. One of them stood open already, having detected that Thatcher's comm was approaching, and they both entered.

Inside, Guerrero stood with her arms draped down her stomach, one hand gripping the other's wrist. She looked at him expectantly.

Thatcher drew several deep breaths. "I can't afford mistakes. Supposing I were to let you return as the *Jersey*'s primary Ops officer…the moment I saw you slip, I'd have to relieve you again. That knowledge alone would prove stressful to you. And if it came to relieving you, I can't see it doing much for your recovery. Yours, or the crew's."

The doors opened onto the headquarters' ground floor with a muted *ding*, and Thatcher sprinted out again, down a corridor that led to the lobby.

Guerrero didn't miss a step, keeping pace with him from the outset. "That's just it, sir. I'm as recovered as I'm going to get. My disposition is my disposition, and as far as I'm concerned, managing my stress is *my* responsibility. Not anyone else's."

Thatcher didn't answer as they raced through the lobby, his brain turning over like an engine as he processed Guerrero's words. More than one head turned to track their rush through the open, brightly lit space. Someone shouted Thatcher's name as they reached the bulletproof glass doors, but he simply couldn't process additional interactions on any level, so he ignored whoever it was.

A decision like reinstating Guerrero…. *That's something I'd normally give a lot of thought to.*

In truth, he should have already thought about it. But in the rush to reach Freedom System from The Brush, and then during the confused chaos of the effort to repel Daybreak from the system, the question of Guerrero simply hadn't crossed his mind.

They reached the self-driving speeder waiting for him at the curb. He placed a hand on the back door's handle.

"Sir?" Guerrero waited beside him, posture whip-straight. She was almost standing at attention.

He squeezed his eyes shut, then released the handle. He met her serious gaze.

"Sir, I can't sit around here anymore. Not when I could be out there protecting Oasis. Protecting my family."

Slowly, he nodded. He could understand that.

Guerrero was clearly trying her best to keep her composure, but the tension around her eyes told him how much this meant to her.

"Spending time around Ron and the kids has been…well, I've enjoyed it more than I can put into words. It's been nice to just be with them, doing things that don't matter at all. Not compared to the things we've done aboard the *Jersey*, anyway." She gave a small, helpless-looking shrug. "That's why I have to get back out there. It's why I have to fight. Because of how precious those moments are. Just doing absolutely nothing, with people I love. If Daybreak wins, no one will ever feel that relaxed and free again. They'll live under the thumb of people who don't care about them—who maybe even hate them. I can't let that happen. Not while I'm still breathing."

Thatcher could understand that sentiment completely. He thought of Lin—which, inexplicably, made him think of Rose. And that reminded him of what he'd done in Clime.

It's so important to have people around you who you can trust.

Against his better judgment, Thatcher grabbed the back door's handle again and opened it. "Get in the speeder."

Guerrero blinked, glanced into the car, then met his eyes. "Sir?"

"Welcome back, Lieutenant."

Tears sprang to Guerrero's eyes, and without warning, she seized him in a tight hug.

He stiffened. This was the sort of familiar gesture he never would have expected from Guerrero. Not in a million years.

Hesitantly, he patted her back, and barely restrained himself from saying "There, there," which would have undoubtedly made this ten times more awkward.

"We'd best be going," he said instead. "In ten minutes, we'll be late for our shuttle."

Guerrero pulled away, smiling, and looking slightly embarrassed. He gave her a tight smile, then gestured toward the open door.

She got in, shifting to the left side of the back seat, and he climbed in after her, shutting the door.

Guerrero was still smiling. "Thank you, sir."

He nodded. "I'll tell you what I told Bill. When it's just us, please feel free to call me Tad."

"Oh. Uh, okay. Tad."

CHAPTER 23

Aboard Attack Shuttle One
Agersia System, The Splay
Earth Year 2291

THATCHER FIGURED DAYBREAK WAS PROBABLY STILL SENSITIVE about Wilson taking Whitherward Trading Station, so he sent a transmission to the *Victorious* suggesting they route the fleet around Scanderoon System

He expected Moll to insist they sail straight through it, if only to demonstrate that he didn't need Thatcher's advice. It seemed like the sort of thing the man might do.

So it surprised him when the reply not only agreed with his suggestion, but also included an invitation to dine with Moll aboard the destroyer while en route to the target system.

I expected Moll to tell *me how the battle will go, not invite me to a chummy dinner to discuss its planning.*

Thatcher didn't trust it. But there was only one way to find out what the man truly intended.

And so here he sat, once again alone aboard Attack Shuttle One, using his eyepiece to study a tactical display patched through from his CIC. It was clear of immediate threats, as it had been since the fleet had entered The Splay.

He switched to the view of the stars offered by one of the shuttle's bow sensors, which faced the Milky Way's core. The wash of white that stretched before him had its usual effect on him: serenity, with a touch of lonely melancholy.

So far, Daybreak had been keeping its distance from the combined Frontier-Sunder force. Once Dirk managed to regroup, he would come at them with everything he had. But for now, they had time.

Commander Becker met him at his shuttle's hatch once more, saluting him curtly. "This way, please. I'm to lead you to the wardroom."

Thatcher nodded, and they set off without another word.

As they progressed through the destroyer's labyrinth of passageways, he realized what it was that he hadn't quite been able to put his finger on during his last visit, concerning the crew. They didn't act like mere employees of Sunder. Each crewmember's air was that of a citizen whose nation he considered superior to all others. They were like the subjects of an empire that had already conquered everything.

Moll rose to his feet as Thatcher entered the wardroom, saluting him.

Another first. Thatcher returned the salute.

"I'm honored you came. Have you met Petty Officer Nolan?" Moll jerked a thumb toward a man waiting nearby, clasping the handle of a trolley bearing various metal food warmers.

"I have not."

Nolan saluted, and Thatcher returned his as well.

"He has prepared a seven-course meal for us this evening, which promises to be exquisite, judging by the smell. Please, have a seat." Moll gestured toward the opposite end of the table where he sat. "Let's not delay."

Thatcher lowered himself into the cushioned chair, which

proved much more comfortable than the heavy, utilitarian things in the *New Jersey*'s wardroom.

With that, Nolan removed the cover from two circular warmers, revealing plates that bore two tarts each.

Thatcher was served first, but he waited until Moll had his before trying it.

Once his plate was in front of him, the Sunder CEO didn't hesitate, stuffing a whole tart into his mouth and then talking around it. "Blue cheese and pear tartlets. My mother used to make these. Go ahead, Commander, I haven't had them poisoned."

Offering a tight smile, Thatcher bit into one of them. The burnt-caramel taste of the blue cheese exploded in his mouth, counterbalancing the pear's sweetness perfectly. He finished chewing, then swallowed, washing it down with some water. "They're delicious."

"Of course they are. As I said, my mother made them. By the way. You didn't tell me Veronica Rose had you iced."

Ah. Thatcher nodded to himself, lowering the rest of the tart to his plate. *This feels more familiar.* "The *New Jersey* was out of commission."

Moll shrugged. "She could have loaned you a different ship while repairs were being conducted, couldn't she? Seems like a sensible gesture, for her most skilled tactician."

He'd placed a slight emphasis on the word "tactician." It reminded Thatcher, as he felt sure it was meant to, of Moll's little oration months ago, as they'd walked through the *Jersey*'s passageways.

Clever tactics may fly in Earth Local Space, Moll had said, *where the mommy state is never too far, ready with its super-ships to swoop in and save the day. But things are different here on the Cluster's outskirts, and tactics will only get you so far. If they're all you're playing with, then sooner or later you'll face an implacable foe who has you right where he wants you. And he will end you.*

Thatcher said nothing, and Moll waved dismissively, as if to suggest the matter should be forgotten. That didn't fool Thatcher. He'd already figured out that Moll forgot nothing.

The man popped his second tart into his mouth. "Dirk is a war criminal," he said around it as he chewed. "There's no doubt about that. A rabid dog in need of euthanizing. But I have to say, there's one thing I agree with him about. Your CEO's notion of 'free space' is utterly untenable. I would use the words comically ridiculous, except I know one is supposed to speak more diplomatically than that to one's treasured allies." He put another slight emphasis on "treasured," which smacked of sarcasm. So this dinner *was* about flaunting his power.

Thatcher met the man's arrogant gaze with a neutral expression. "Free space is about nothing more than maintaining basic freedoms. The same freedoms that were fought for hundreds of years ago by the nations that rose out of Earth's West. Yes, those freedoms have been trampled on in recent centuries. But Rose is fighting to bring them back. You come from a Western country. Shouldn't you want the same thing?"

Smiling, Moll shook his head. "Your naivete continues to astound me, Commander. Look around you. Conditions in the Cluster leave no room for the freedoms you mention."

Thatcher pressed his lips together. "If you truly believe that, then maybe you're the next one we'll need to take down."

Moll studied Thatcher's face for a moment, then burst into hearty laughter. "I won't bother reminding you that Sunder is the only reason Frontier still exists," he said once his mirth began to fade. "As to your threat, I'll just say this. For your sake, I hope it doesn't come to that."

"Tell me the purpose of the mining ships and freighters you've brought with you." No one had asked that question during the board room meeting at Frontier headquarters. Either they hadn't thought it worth asking, or hadn't dared. But Thatcher did dare, and he didn't trust Moll the slightest bit.

"Wait and see, Commander. You will learn things as you need to learn them. So you should expect to learn them at quite a late stage."

With that, Thatcher stood, having heard enough. "We're finished here. We can discuss what battle plans you'll deign to discuss with me via comms."

"As you wish. Thank you so much for joining me, Commander Thatcher. I trust you can find your own way to your shuttle?"

Thatcher gave a curt nod, then strode through the hatch, leaving most of the first course uneaten on his plate. The taste of blue cheese lingered in his mouth, however, and he resolved to wash it down with coffee the moment he returned to the *Jersey*.

CHAPTER 24

Aboard the *New Jersey*
Bakelite System, The Splay
Earth Year 2291

THE *JERSEY* LEAPT INTO THE BAKELITE JUMP ZONE, AND Thatcher found himself holding his breath while he waited for the sensors to populate his holoscreen with data.

Get it together. He forced himself to inhale deeply, then exhale, focusing only on the passage of air through his nostrils.

He'd been on edge ever since leaving Dupliss and entering The Splay. It wasn't merely the fact of sailing through enemy territory—he'd done that often enough in his career. It was jumping from system to system with an 'ally' who he didn't remotely trust.

As they'd flown through the region, he couldn't stop himself from constantly checking the Sunder fleet's posture, though there never seemed to be any cause for alarm.

In contrast, the Daybreak Combine was definitely acting alarmed. As the Frontier-Sunder force progressed through their territory, they seemed to piece together where it was going, which Thatcher supposed wasn't hard to do. Strategically, Bakelite was the most important system for at least ten light years in every direction. And Frontier had a recent history of destroying vital mineral refineries. Identifying Isovol and Isopor Stations as their goal—Bakelite's twin refineries—didn't take much genius.

As they'd neared the destination system, Guerrero had spotted scout ships flitting through systems ahead of them, and their own scouts reported significant ship movements through the surrounding systems.

Some level of resistance will await us in Bakelite, Thatcher had concluded. *All that's left to learn is how much.*

After the titanic battle in Freedom System, it seemed unlikely that Daybreak had managed to regroup enough to do more than bolster Bakelite's defenses.

Either way, he was about to find out.

Guerrero's fingers danced across her console, her holoscreen flashing as she flicked between applets, moving information around at breakneck speeds. "Sir, I'm detecting a battle group of eleven Daybreak warships—two destroyers, three light armored cruisers, two frigates, three logistics ships, and one eWar ship. I've found matches in the *Jersey*'s database for all but one of the cruisers and two logistics ships. Sending the specs to your console now."

"Acknowledged, Lieutenant." Then, Thatcher made himself add: "Thank you."

Getting Guerrero back in his CIC had proven to be a…mixed blessing. She was clearly trying her best to be even more meticulous than before.

Another captain would have rejoiced at that. But it only made Thatcher nervous, because he knew she was only doing it to prove herself to him. He needed her motivation to stem from victory.

Some would call that a trivial distinction, but there *was* a distinction. Keeping up appearances wasn't the same thing as sheer effectiveness.

She's just rusty, he told himself. *She'll come back to us. The old Guerrero will come back. She just needs time.*

Time I hope I can afford to give her.

Thatcher paged through the data she'd sent until they neared the Daybreak force's coordinates. As he'd expected, the enemy commander was competent enough to position his battle group outside the loose ring of five jump gates that orbited Bakelite's star. If he'd remained within the ring, Thatcher and Moll would have easily surrounded his force.

Almost on cue, Guerrero spoke again. "Sunder ships are entering the system through the other jump gates, sir, as well as our other Frontier ships. It appears we've synchronized our movements successfully."

Thatcher nodded. Along with Bakelite's wealth of minerals, and its twin refineries positioned equidistant between the jump gates and the asteroid belt, the system's ring of jump gates served as another feature that contributed massively to its value. They were much closer to each other than in most systems, a feat enabled by the fact they followed off-ecliptic orbits.

Because of this arrangement, the system's asteroid belt didn't interfere with ships jumping in and out. Except for twice per year, per jump gate—when its orbit would bring it in line with the belt. But any northern captain worth his salt kept a chart on file that allowed him to track the orbits of Bakelite's jump gates and navigate through the system in a safe and timely manner.

The gates' close proximity to each other facilitated not only swift export of refined materials, but also a quick trip through what was already a crossroads system.

All of which was to say, taking Bakelite would *definitely* piss off Herwin Dirk.

Thatcher tapped on his holoscreen, closely examining the sensor data Guerrero had forwarded, to make sure this situation did indeed match one of the scenarios he and Moll had projected. The man had apparently decided Thatcher was worth consulting when it came to taking Bakelite. Over comms, they'd gone over multiple scenarios for how this engagement might play out, and this was one of them.

But Thatcher still had no idea what the plan was for *after* they'd taken the system.

He cleared his throat before tapping the armrest panel to put himself over the command channel. "We're following Battle Plan Epsilon, everyone." Upon his return to Freedom, he'd been pleased to find his ideas for fleet integration were seeing rapid implementation. It would take more time for his vision to be fully realized, but this was an excellent start. The *Jersey* had undergone the upgrade to her comms while he'd been planetside —and so had several Sunder ships, though it had pained Veronica Rose to share the innovation with Moll. She'd had no choice, since it could prove critical to this mission's success. The remaining Sunder ships had been working on upgrading their comms in transit.

"EWar ships, join your counterparts in jamming the enemy's sensors as you shoot past them on both their flanks. All corvettes, you are to escort the combined eWar squadron past the enemy formation. You will be joined by a proportionate number of logistics ships. Please indicate that you've heard and understood."

His command applet lit up green as the other Frontier ships acknowledged his orders. Each captain would have received every projected scenario, as well as the battle plans that accompanied them, and Thatcher knew they'd almost certainly memorized them. But he believed in leaving nothing to chance, and so he intended to give every order as though none of them knew what it would be.

The eWar-led forces snaked around the enemy battle group, blinding them in sensor fog. As expected, however, the effect was short-lived. In addition to keeping his ships outside the ring of jump gates, the Daybreak commander had also positioned them near the Isovol Refinery, allowing them to avail of the station's sensor array, on top of their own countermeasures.

Confusion reigned aboard the enemy ships for no more than twenty seconds. After that, they began to fire on the Frontier squadrons sailing past their flanks.

In the heat of battle, Thatcher hammered his console with his index finger, harder than he'd meant to. "All damage dealers fire primary lasers on the pair of targets I'm designating. Guerrero, forward our targeting data to the *Victorious*."

"Aye, sir."

Moll had agreed that under such a scenario, where they outnumbered the enemy almost three-to-one, they could afford to divide their fire between at least three targets while still ensuring they went down quickly.

Blue beams shot across the tactical display, connecting with the trio of enemy logistics ships. Thatcher brought up a visual on his holoscreen to watch their shields shudder and buck. He had no access to their actual power readouts, but over the years he'd learned to estimate how close the forcefields were to failing.

There, he thought, staring at the middle logistics vessel. *That one will go first.*

The shield flickered out of existence, and the concentrated laserfire extended past to land on the target's hull, immediately scoring it.

He was about to call for Hellborns, but didn't bother. The enemy ship was small enough that the enormous amount of energy being dumped into her was more than enough to make her pop.

Indeed, the logistics ship ruptured just as its counterpart's shields went down, followed by the third's.

With all three of its logistics vessels gone, the enemy force was left vulnerable, and its commander knew it. Within seconds, they began broadcasting their surrender.

"Sir, we're getting a transmission from the *Victorious*. It's Captain Moll."

Thatcher restrained a grimace. Moll had Frontier over a barrel, and by extension, he had Thatcher in the same position. The CIC crew knew that, but even so, Thatcher hated having conversations with the smug CEO in front of them. He felt sure it did nothing for his crew's morale.

Moll's head and shoulders appeared in the holotank at the front of the CIC. Enlarged as it was, his face's lines and contours were thrown into sharp relief. For the first time since they'd left Dupliss, Thatcher noticed just how tired the man looked.

Moll wasted no time in dispensing orders. Even that was enough to annoy Thatcher—the assumption that he was Moll's subordinate, and that he would follow any orders he gave.

Which, of course, he would. What else could he do?

"I'm leaving your battle group in charge of securing the surrendered ships," Moll said. "They'll prove useful for system defense."

Thatcher nodded. "Speaking of that, are you ready to discuss our plans for defending Bakelite?"

A small grin sprouted on Moll's lips. "For now, I want you to patrol the jump gates. I'll lend you my scout ships—send them and yours to the connecting systems, with orders to return to Bakelite and report any potential threats."

"What will you do?"

"I have business in the belt."

With that, Moll cut off the transmission, eliciting a round of fidgeting from Thatcher's CIC crew. They liked being in the dark about as much as he did.

Guerrero spoke up. "Sir, the Sunder ships are leaving."

Thatcher blinked. "Which Sunder ships?"

"Most of their destroyers, and…yes, looks like their mining

ships are going too, along with the construction ships, and the freighters. Their scouts appear to be staying, just as Captain Moll said, and a few warships. The rest of the Sunder fleet is headed for the Bakelite asteroid belt."

Thatcher watched the procession on the tactical display. Moll's ships all seemed to be headed for the same region of the belt. He made a mental note to see what was available in the public record about the Bakelite asteroid belt's resource distribution. Specifically in the section Moll was sailing toward.

Over half our force just left us. And I still have no idea what the hell is going on.

<h1 style="text-align:center">CHAPTER 25</h1>

Aboard the *New Jersey*
Bakelite System, The Splay
Earth Year 2291

THATCHER HATED EVERY PART OF THIS MISSION.

He hated the way the days blended into one another. That already happened easily enough aboard a starship, where the closest thing to night was when you turned off the overhead lights before falling asleep in your bunk. During the 'day'—and each watch's day happened at different times, so that in truth the ship was stuck in an unending daytime—the soft UVB lights in the passageways did their best to mimic the sun, even triggering vitamin D synthesis in the skin.

He hated the unending tension of knowing an attack was coming, eventually, but not when. The way that tension exhibited itself in sharp words, twitches, and in Thatcher's case, a stiff neck.

Most of all, he hated not having control. Since being given the *New Jersey* as his first command, he hadn't realized how accustomed he'd become to being in control. Not until it was taken away from him.

"Sir, a Sunder freighter is leaving the asteroid belt. Judging by her trajectory, she appears to be headed for Isopor."

As he'd had to countless times since beginning their endless patrols, Thatcher suppressed an urge to tell Guerrero that he didn't need to know every detail about Sunder's movements. "Thank you, Lieutenant," he said instead.

Out of everyone aboard the *Jersey*, Guerrero seemed the most anxious about having little to do. She'd taken to giving Thatcher updates on the slightest sign of Sunder activity in the asteroid belt, whether it was a mining ship making a brief appearance during its journey between asteroids, a construction ship flitting in and out of view, a freighter hauling raw materials to one of the refineries, or the same freighter taking refined metals back out to the belt a day or two later.

Ultimately, he decided that having as much intel as possible on Moll's activities was probably a good thing. Yes, the most important reports were those the scouts brought back hourly from the surrounding systems. But so far, those had remained consistently boring, with no sign of approaching threats. Whatever Moll was doing in the belt, however, both intrigued and worried him.

What are they building out there?

Isopor Station specialized in refining hydrogen, helium, and oxygen. Isovol was used for nickel, iron, magnesium, platinum, and gold. Most of Moll's freighters went to Isovol when they came in-system, but a significant number went to Isopor.

"Sir?"

Thatcher's eyes snapped to the Ops officer's open, honest face, and he pressed his lips together to catch the testy remark threatening to emerge. "Yes, Guerrero?"

"Our weapons officer contacted me again about replenishing railgun ammunition in advance of the next engagement. We're also running low on powdered eggs, powdered milk, and pancake mix, along with a number of condiments."

Thatcher nodded. Gregory Horton, the *Jersey*'s chief weapons officer, had a certain expectation for the ship's ammunition stores. If they fell below a certain level, he got antsy, which resulted in an unending barrage of notices to Guerrero, who passed them on to Thatcher.

For his part, Thatcher knew they had enough ammunition to last two somewhat lengthy engagements at least. But their munitions had fallen below Horton's magic threshold, and so the man would remain aggravating until they obtained more.

It was Thatcher's usual habit to ignore the weapons officer until they actually needed to restock, since UNREPs—underway replenishments—were tedious affairs and best avoided if at all possible. But their depleting powdered egg supplies pushed him to seriously consider the idea. Yes, they could survive without eggs, along with the other things Guerrero had mentioned. But the crew's morale was already stretched paper-thin, and food had a surprising effect in that regard. Especially when it was food the crew had come to expect daily.

Okay. Decision made. He had Guerrero begin contacting her counterparts aboard the other Frontier and Sunder ships that were also patrolling the system's jump zones.

A surprisingly short amount of time had passed when she turned from her console to face him. "Sir, the Sunder destroyer *Archimedes* has agreed to replenish the needed ammunition and supplies."

Thatcher raised his eyebrows. Securing an UNREP normally required no end of favor-trading, ego-massaging, and outright begging. The fact that this captain, whoever he was, had agreed so readily…. "Who captains *Archimedes*, Lieutenant?"

"Captain Boris Redding, sir."

"Then send Captain Redding my thanks."

He spent the next better part of an hour coordinating with his

Nav, Helm, and Ops officers—as well as their counterparts aboard the *Archimedes*—to get the *Jersey*'s starboard side in line with the destroyer's port, at a distance of just a few kilometers. It always made Thatcher uneasy to bring his ship in such close proximity to another. Amidst the great vastness of space, at this distance they might as well have been touching hulls.

Getting into position wouldn't be the end of it, either. While shuttles flew back and forth between the warships, the two CIC crews would need to continue coordinating to ensure the ships' orbits remained synced, which involved managing minute, ongoing differentials in acceleration, trajectory, and thruster activity.

By the time the first shuttle launched from the destroyer, laden with goods for the cruiser, Thatcher had developed a twitch in his left eye. Adding to his stress was the necessity to keep his demeanor calm and pleasant while interacting with his crew, and especially with the CIC crew of the destroyer. Nothing would hurt his chances of future UNREPs more than letting his irritation show during the current one.

After the third of five shuttles had docked with the *Jersey*'s forward starboard cargo bay, Thatcher noticed that Guerrero had stopped whatever she'd been doing to read something on her holoscreen.

"What is it, Guerrero?"

"It's somewhat strange, sir…Captain Redding wants to meet with you."

"Meet with me? Isn't he in the *Archimedes*' CIC?"

"Apparently that's his XO."

"But he introduced himself as Redding."

"Apparently…" Guerrero swallowed. "Apparently that wasn't truthful. Apparently the real Captain Redding has come aboard the *New Jersey* via the shuttle that just docked with us, and wishes to meet you."

Thatcher exchanged glances with Bill Candle, who'd twisted

in the XO's chair to face him. Candle looked just as bemused as Thatcher felt.

"Very well. You have the conn, XO."

With that, Thatcher rose and left the CIC, running his hands over the front of his uniform to smooth it out, though it was impeccably pressed.

Captain Boris Redding stood near the newly arrived shuttle, which the *Jersey* deck crew were in the process of unloading. Men wove around the destroyer captain carrying stacked cases of dried fruit, jerky, energy bars, and all manner of preserved goods.

Does he realize he's standing right in their way?

"Captain Redding." Thatcher snapped to attention in front of the visiting commander, offering a salute. The man was technically his superior.

"Commander." Redding returned the salute.

"Let's go back to my office, where we can have a discussion without so much…bustle." Thatcher gestured faintly at one of the deck crew, who nearly collided with Redding's backside, then blinked rapidly at the captain standing statuesque in front of the shuttle's airlock before maneuvering around him with a box of canned peaches.

"Your office is close?"

"Uh, no. It's near the CIC." That was fairly standard warship design, making Redding's question an odd one. *He seems flustered.*

"There isn't time, then. Only two shuttle trips remain in the UNREP. I have to return with the final one. Is there somewhere closer we can meet?"

"Um." Thatcher turned on his heel, scanning the cargo bay and searching his cluttered brain. He was keen to get Redding out of the way. "There." He pointed to a maintenance closet opposite the docking bay.

Once inside the closet, Redding eyed the tool-filled shelves warily before turning to face Thatcher wearing a somewhat strained expression. "Shut the hatch."

Thatcher had a bad feeling about this. Was it wise to enclose himself with a Sunder ship captain, alone in a closet, when he hadn't told anyone where he was going?

One of the crew had to notice us coming in here. Their captain ducking into a maintenance closet and closing the hatch behind him seemed like the kind of thing the crew would notice. Besides, he felt fairly certain he could handle Redding if it came to blows.

He shut the hatch, then crossed the closet to lean against a work bench. As he did, his hand strayed close to a rack that held wrenches of various sizes. If the man tried anything, Thatcher would throw one of the tools at his head. It seemed as good a plan as any.

"Can I ask why you hid yourself amongst the freeze-dried ice cream instead of simply arranging a visit?"

"Because if I visited officially, Moll would know."

"Right," Thatcher said, as though he understood, which he didn't. After a few seconds' silence, he decided to confess his ignorance. "Why does that matter?"

"He's the reason I'm visiting. I'm here to tell you not to trust him."

"Then I'm afraid you went to a lot of wasted effort, Captain. There's no one I trust less than Simon Moll."

"It wasn't wasted. Believe me when I say you don't know anything about Moll. No one does. Rumors say he killed Patrick Moen. Moen was Sunder's first CEO."

"I know who Patrick Moen was." Moen had been a friend of Thatcher's grandfather. "Though I don't put much stock in rumors."

"Moll would scare me even without the rumors. Haven't you noticed the way he behaves?"

Like an asshole? "What are you referring to, exactly?"

"He knows things he shouldn't. Like when enemy forces might be waiting in the next system. Without scouting it first."

"Couldn't that come from simply having intelligence on their movements?"

Redding shook his head. "No one has this level of intel. Moll often knows not just their presence, but their fleet's posture, and he's almost always right. And the way he looks at you…like he knows more about you than you know about yourself. Like he's always ten steps ahead of you."

"I haven't noticed that, actually."

"Well, that's just it." Redding nodded, as if to punctuate his own point. "He doesn't act that way about you, Commander. I think you scare him. He considers you a threat. That's why I wanted to come here. To warn you to watch your back. Sooner or later, Moll removes threats."

Silence followed Redding's words, as Thatcher took a moment to digest them. *So even Moll's own employees are worried about his power play.* "If you feel that way, then why don't you just quit Sunder?"

"That's easy, Commander Thatcher. The only thing more frightening than being near Moll is being on the side opposing him."

With that, Redding crossed the closet and brushed past Thatcher to open the hatch and peek outside.

He glanced back to meet Thatcher's eyes. "I'll leave now. The less time I'm away from my CIC, the less likely it will be that Moll figures this out."

Without another word, Redding hurried out into the cargo bay, leaving Thatcher alone in the maintenance closet with his thoughts.

CHAPTER 26

New Houston, Oasis Colony
Freedom System, Dupliss Region
Earth Year 2291

ROSE AND MITTELMAN WALKED SIDE-BY-SIDE THROUGH Frontier's R&D department, which took up three subbasements in the HQ's main building.

The department lacked "corridors" as such. Instead, the connecting areas held common working spaces, where the company's engineers could collaborate on difficult projects rather than remain siloed and toiling in frustrated isolation.

It was Gregory Rose's design—her late father's—and Rose had never seen it used so well. Nanofab tech's implementation had every Frontier scientist and techie going full-tilt, and they were only in the beginning stages.

The atmosphere down here was a world apart from the HQ's upper levels. Up there, stressed-out executives and office workers buzzed about, on-edge from the titanic battle that had so recently rent Oasis' skies…and constantly aware that another one could come at any moment, almost without warning.

Whether it was Daybreak Combine from above, or the Xanthic from below, the people of Oasis lived with a level of fear unrivaled throughout the rest of the Cluster, as far as Rose could tell from the chatter on the instant comms net. And yet, down here, the researchers seemed exuberant.

Their conversations were punctuated by wild gesticulation, and voices that rose over one another's as each argued for their philosophy of implementation. But there was no anger or irritation—only passionate energy.

Rose envied them that.

Mittelman spoke, breaking the gap in their own conversation, which had stretched on for at least thirty seconds now. "I've been thinking."

She gave a small smile. "And the Cluster trembles."

"Huh?" The spymaster shot her a quizzical look.

"It was a joke." She shook her head. "Never mind."

"Right." He cleared his throat. "I've been thinking we can expand the concept of free space. The idea of free space versus closed space…lately, I've been comparing it to public versus private military recruitment."

Tilting her head, Rose tried to discern the connection. She failed. "You have?"

"Yes. You don't see the parallels? Government-run militaries will take all comers, so long as each recruit passes the requisite physical and medical exams and loves his country. But PMCs only want to hire people already trained by national militaries."

Rose nodded. "It's how we stay profitable. Antimatter reactors aren't cheap, and neither are hulls, or pressure suits, weapons, ammunition, food…and everything else it takes to run a small military. We can't afford to invest millions in training programs on top of all that."

"We can't afford it right now. But nanofabbers will bring down some of the costs you just mentioned. Way down."

Rose inspected her Chief Intelligence Officer's face. "What are you getting at?"

"With the wormhole closed, our supply of spacers trained on the public dime—like our dear friend Commander Thatcher, for instance—has dried up. Who will crew our nanofabbed ships? Who will fight in those ships' marine detachments, or those big enough to have detachments, anyway? There are only so many Frederick Wilsons who'll be interested in coming out of retirement. And most of those, we'd likely want to remain retired."

"You've certainly outlined the problem, Hans. Now let's hear the solution."

"A mass training program. We welcome comers from all over the Cluster. Just like, under free space, anyone is invited to visit or live within Frontier space—so will anyone be invited to apply for a job, and be trained by us. To join the ranks of the Cluster's most competent warriors." Mittelman smiled, though his smile faltered when he turned it on Rose, and no doubt noticed her expression. Still, he pressed on: "Who wouldn't want to fight for such an inspiring company? One who actually takes a stand for what's right?"

Rose reflected on her decision to hire Celeste Security Solutions, and the decision to use Oasis' Helio bases in combat—losing four of the six in the process. She thought about the things she'd allowed herself to do in service of what she believed was right, and the knowledge that she would do worse, if it came to that. Did achieving free space justify what she was doing in its name?

"Frontier has standards, Hans. Not everyone has what it takes to be one of our employees. And it's not just about military experience. It's physical excellence. It's the ability to think on your feet. Problem solving. Passion. Vision. Leadership."

"Any more buzz words you care to add?"

Rose gave a dry chuckle. "They're not just buzz words here,

Hans. If I wasn't sincere about hiring only the best, do you think I'd have the most effective CIO in the Cluster?"

That drew a smile from the spymaster.

There's nothing like a little flattery to get him to lighten up. "There's also still the issue of cost. Even if I was willing to relax our standards, which I'm not—developing a 'mass training program,' as you put it, wouldn't be cheap. Neither is hiring the necessary trainers, constructing new barracks and training grounds, or absorbing the liability of having substandard candidates running wild all over our facilities. I won't have Frontier become the face of laxness. Or of chaos."

"Chaos may be what we need right now."

She shook her head emphatically. "It's not how I was raised."

Mittelman emitted a frustrated sigh. "You could cover the costs by expanding. Into other systems, and regions."

"Like Sunder is?"

He shrugged. "Moll does have a point, Veronica, bastard that he is. Expansion *has* become necessary, in today's Dawn Cluster."

"Then we'll expand by negotiating deals with the free people of each system. Mining rights in exchange for protection. Use of shipyards and refineries in exchange for security. Housing and recreation for our employees in exchange for service. All offered and traded freely, without coercion. And," she added, raising a finger to emphasize her point, "we will hire only the Cluster's elite. It's interesting that you bring up Sunder to make your point, actually, considering they also only employ the best. If we ever found ourselves on the opposite side of a battlespace from them under your plan, we'd lose."

Mittelman seemed like he wanted to say more, but he had to see Rose wasn't going to budge on this.

"Very well," he said, before changing the subject to trends developing in the Cluster's south, passed on to him by his operatives there.

CHAPTER 27

Aboard the *New Jersey*
Bakelite System, The Splay
Earth Year 2291

"Sir, the *Victorious* has emerged from the asteroid belt and is moving down-system. Four other Sunder destroyers are accompanying her, along with eight eWar vessels."

"Acknowledged." Thatcher watched the oddly composed battle group creep across the system display on his holoscreen. It would take hours for them to reach the ring of jump gates where the *New Jersey* and the other ships were patrolling, but even so, he'd like to know what they were up to. Why move down-system with so many damage dealers, when the jump zones were already secure? The scouts they'd deployed to the five connecting systems had orders to return and alert Thatcher to anything that resembled an approaching threat.

"Send the *Victorious* an encrypted transmission requesting an update." That seemed more likely to get an answer out of Moll, rather than demanding an explanation for his behavior over an open channel.

"Aye, sir." Guerrero's fingers tapped smartly at her console.

Their watch had been due to end fifteen minutes after his Ops officer had spotted the approaching Sunder ships, but Thatcher decided to extend it at least until Moll enlightened him as to his actions. He allowed his CIC crew to leave one at a time, to use the head or grab a coffee from the wardroom if they desired. He didn't normally allow beverages inside the CIC, but that was largely as a precaution against the possibility they'd need to make sudden maneuvers. In such a circumstance, coffee spilling across consoles would be the last thing they needed. But that didn't seem likely, today.

And yet, Moll's reasons for visiting the system's core remained a mystery. Thatcher returned from the wardroom toting a lidded coffee of his own to learn that the *Victorious* and her traveling partners had passed Isopor Station without responding to the *Jersey*'s transmission. They'd had more than enough time to receive and understand it, and yet there was utter silence over the comms.

Bryce Sullivan, Thatcher's Nav officer, spoke up. "Sir, their trajectory has them on an intercept course with this group of Sunder ships." He circled something on his console, and a red line appeared on Thatcher's tactical display as well, enveloping a destroyer, a light armored cruiser, two frigates, and a logistics ship.

The destroyer was the *Archimedes*—the same one that had performed an UNREP for the *Jersey*, and whose captain had paid him a secret visit during it.

"Set a course that takes us near those ships at the same time the *Victorious* reaches them," Thatcher said.

"Aye, sir."

He didn't know what Moll was up to, but he did know he wanted to be within real-time comms range—and within weapons range. The chances of this coming to blows seemed vanishingly small, but having a cruiser's suite of weaponry staring you down did go a long way toward keeping people honest, Thatcher had discovered.

As the *Victorious* and the *New Jersey* converged on the patrolling group of Sunder ships, shields flickered to life around the *Archimedes*, and only the *Archimedes*.

Odd.

"Sir, the *Archimedes*—"

"I see it, Lieutenant. Very strange."

Why hadn't the other ships put their shields up? Had Moll threatened Captain Redding directly? Or did Redding know to expect danger?

As if to answer Thatcher's questions, primary lasers lanced out from all five approaching destroyers, slamming into Redding's forcefield and causing it to shudder wildly.

Shocked silence reigned throughout the *New Jersey*'s CIC. Tim Ortega shot a furtive glance in Thatcher's direction from the Tactical station, and on Thatcher's right, Billy Candle had gone stiff in the XO's chair.

When Thatcher tried to speak, his voice came out a hoarse whisper. "Guerrero. Any response from the *Victorious*?"

She met his eyes from the Ops station, looking helpless. "None, Captain."

The logistics ship flying in formation with the *Archimedes* made no attempt to bolster her shields via microwave beam, and indeed, all four ships accompanying her decelerated and then reversed course, distancing themselves from the destroyer.

The great vessel's shield faltered, then failed. All five beams extended to land on her hull, and for a moment Thatcher thought Moll was going to burn her from space. But the primary laserfire ceased all at once, leaving a scorched and twisted hull, and the five destroyers switched to secondaries, using them to pinpoint the hull-mounted railgun turrets facing them and melting battery after battery to slag.

Once the last battery positioned to oppose them had been

melted, the five attacking destroyers launched two shuttles each, which Thatcher assumed were stuffed to capacity with marines.

"Try contacting the *Archimedes*' CIC." Thatcher doubted that would amount to much, but he had to do something.

Guerrero began to carry out his order, but her hands flew from her console in frustration. "The eWar ships accompanying the *Victorious* started jamming our comms the moment I attempted to contact *Archimedes*, sir. It's like they were waiting for us to try."

Thatcher gritted his teeth. Against eight jamming eWar ships, no countermeasures would clear his comms—not until Moll wanted them cleared. If he'd had enough eWar vessels with the *Jersey* to rival their number, or the advantage of a nearby sensor platform, things would have been different. As things stood, there would be no communicating with Boris Redding. Unless Moll decided to permit it, and Thatcher had significant doubts about that happening.

You need to do something, he told himself. But what? He found himself wondering what his grandfather would have done. Would Edward Thatcher have spotted a possible action that his grandson couldn't see? Some way to put a stop to this madness?

Moll had obviously kept him in the dark intentionally, and he knew that for Thatcher to oppose him would be disastrous. The *Jersey* was the only Frontier ship within firing range, and even if his comms were clear to contact the others, they wouldn't get here until whatever was happening had ended.

Should I have called them to join us while we were sailing here? As a precaution?

That would have been ill-advised, too. Not only was Sunder's force in Bakelite much larger than Frontier's, but even supposing Thatcher managed to defeat Moll, he'd still be deep inside enemy territory without allies. Herwin Dirk was no doubt marshaling his forces around Bakelite at this very moment, and a focused assault on the system was coming. It was a question of when, not if.

If Thatcher opposed Moll here, it wouldn't just be ruinous for the Frontier crews under his command. It would also spell the end for Frontier Security as a whole.

There was nothing he could do. Nothing, except watch as Moll did whatever he wanted.

Yet another flagrant display of his power. Word of this will travel to the edges of the Cluster and back again.

And that, Thatcher realized, was likely the point. Part of it, anyway. Moll had been the first to talk about propaganda as the most powerful weapon of all, in the wake of the wormhole's collapse. But his style of propaganda was clearly nothing like that of Veronica Rose.

Where she presented herself as an idealistic freedom fighter, Moll was developing his own brand into something different, and much darker. An image built on fear and intimidation. All delivered with a self-assured sneer.

During the long minutes that followed, Thatcher felt more ineffective and foolish than he ever had in his life. He felt foolish for trusting Moll—for going deep into the Cluster's south and seeking this alliance. And for helping Moll to do whatever it was he intended to do, here in Bakelite.

No doubt making him feel that way was part of the point. It was how Moll kept those around him unsure of themselves. Off-balance. While Thatcher felt confident he could best Moll at tactics, the man was leagues ahead of him when it came to gaining power, and wielding it. In the long run, that would likely prove to be the more important skill.

After thirty-two minutes, Guerrero spoke up again. "The shuttles Captain Moll sent are undocking with the *Archimedes*, sir. Our comms appear to be clearing."

"Get me Moll." Thatcher's voice came out flat, emotionless.

Guerrero shook her head at whatever her holoscreen was

showing her. "The Ops officer aboard the *Victorious* says Moll is occupied with other matters."

"Tell them I want to know the *Archimedes'* captain and crew are safe."

Nodding, Guerrero typed in the text transmission, and sat with her fingers on the console as she waited for the reply.

It didn't take long. When it came, her eyes widened.

"Sir, according to this, Captain Redding was killed while resisting arrest."

Gasps from all around the CIC. Candle's hand flew to his throat, and he looked like he was going to be sick.

Thatcher heard only his own pulse pounding in his ears.

CHAPTER 28

Aboard the *New Jersey*
Bakelite System, The Splay
Earth Year 2291

MOLL REFUSED TO DISCUSS THE DETAILS SURROUNDING Redding's death until Thatcher was in his office, with no one else present.

The Sunder captain smirked from the desk's holoscreen. "I'm not interested in your attempts to put me on trial in front of your crew, Commander—attempts I'm sure you'd love to make."

Before initiating this meeting, Thatcher had contacted Veronica Rose using the *New Jersey*'s instant comm. Moll's actions had shocked her too, but ultimately she'd come to the same conclusion as Thatcher. As dirty as it made her feel, they still needed Moll.

Hopefully accepting this devil's help doesn't doom us all in the end.

Thatcher's voice came out hard and cold. "Why did you do it?"

"Simple. Redding wasn't playing the same game as the rest of us."

"What game is that?"

The smirk broadened into a sly grin. "Why don't you tell me?"

Thatcher kept his features neutral as he withstood Moll's piercing gaze. The conversation with Redding inside the cargo bay maintenance closet replayed in his head. The man's warnings about what Moll was capable of…and what it had cost him to deliver those warnings.

The murderer allowed the silence to stretch on long enough to make his point. With that, he launched into full cover-up mode. "Some time ago, it came to the attention of our executive that Boris Redding was using his hold to smuggle southern munitions. The c-suite decided to do nothing, giving Redding enough rope to hang himself. Recently, one of our scout ship captains was caught trying to negotiate the sale of those munitions with a Daybreak outrider. Such a deal would have been fine when we were allies with Daybreak Combine, but on the day that alliance fell apart, Redding was stuck with a cargo bay filled with weapons and ammo. On that day, the munitions became contraband. And yet Redding still tried to make the sale."

It tasted like bullshit to Thatcher. Even so, he felt sure Moll would be able to provide him with all the evidence he could want, carefully fabricated and planted to resist all but the most comprehensive scrutiny.

The man was almost daring Thatcher to launch an investigation. The mere act of beginning to investigate would strain ties between Frontier and Sunder. Actually finding evidence of wrongdoing would shatter their partnership, and Frontier would be left alone and vulnerable to its legion of enemies.

But even if Thatcher caught him out, and even if he was willing to sacrifice their alliance…what could he do to bring Moll to justice? With the wormhole's collapse, the Dawn Cluster had truly become humanity's new frontier, and now they had to deal with everything that went with it. The lawlessness. The survival of the most ruthless.

To rally the Cluster and defy the Xanthic, we need order. Unity. Instead, we're fragmenting more every day.

His comm buzzed from the desk beside the holoscreen, and Thatcher picked it up to read the message its screen displayed.

It was from Candle. "Sir, Lieutenant Guerrero has reported that the *Victorious* and the ships accompanying her are moving away from us, back toward the asteroid belt. At their current acceleration profile, they'll be out of real-time comms range in ten minutes."

Thatcher looked from the message to Moll's mirth-filled eyes. "You're leaving."

"Correct. I have matters to attend to in the belt. But I think we both know we're finished here. Don't we, Commander?"

Without answering, Thatcher severed the connection and rose from his chair, striding briskly around the desk to exit his office.

"What's the latest from the *Archimedes*?" he asked as he settled into the command seat minutes later.

Candle cleared his throat, and when he spoke, his voice hitched slightly. "An XO was sent to command her from another Sunder destroyer, the *Hoplite*. Her name is Delphine Contos."

"I see." *Handpicked by Moll himself, I'm sure.* Thatcher wouldn't count on any further warnings or special help from the *Archimedes*.

"Sir—" Guerrero said, then cut off, her voice sounding even more choked than Candle's. She turned toward him, her face drained of color. "Daybreak ships are entering the system through the jump zone out of Halfpace System."

Thatcher's gaze was riveted to his Ops officer's eyes. "How did they get past our scouts?"

"I—I don't know, Captain. They're coming out of the Over-slaugh System jump zone now as well."

In the space of sixty seconds, Daybreak ships began pouring into every jump zone in Bakelite—all five of them filling up with enemy ships.

"Guerrero, send Moll a transmission telling him we need him to turn his destroyers around and help us fight this incursion."

When the reply came, the effect it had on Thatcher's CIC crew was palpable. Shoulders slumped as breath released in long exhales.

Thatcher fought to steel himself, suddenly a lot less certain his people would make it through this day alive.

"Help is on the way," Moll said in the recorded message, and for once his face was free of any smirk or sneer. He radiated only confidence and poise from the holotank. "Until it arrives, I'll need you to protect the refineries. Good luck."

It wasn't difficult to glean the true meaning behind Moll's words.

He's not turning around. We're on our own.

CHAPTER 29

Aboard the *New Jersey*
Bakelite System, The Splay
Earth Year 2291

MOLL HAD TOLD THATCHER TO PROTECT THE REFINERIES —plural.

The idea that the Sunder CEO thought him capable of defending *both* Isovol and Isopor struck him as a strange sort of compliment. To think he could pull that off with his paltry patrolling force was an absurd notion. Even if the Sunder destroyers had stuck around, he doubted it would have been possible.

Regardless, he had no intentions of attempting it.

Tapping the panel built into his command seat's armrest, he spoke over the fleetwide command channel. "All ships form up between Isopor Station and the jump zone out of Halfpace. Do not let the enemy intercept you—if necessary, break with the ecliptic to avoid them." He drew a breath, letting that sink in for a moment. "I'm expecting stealthed ships. All Ops officers should be on high alert for enemy projectiles with no apparent source. The earlier you can track such projectiles, the better our data will be for extrapolating the attacking ship's source."

Could their stealth tech be that advanced? He had no idea. None of them did. They didn't even understand their ally's stealth tech, since Kibishii still refused to share it. Who knew what Meridian might have.

He felt sure that Meridian was responsible for his scouts' failure to report Daybreak's advance on Bakelite. If Meridian's stealth ships had managed to get inside close-in firing range without tipping off the scout ships' captains, they would have stood no chance.

If the Seer-class scout ships had had Kibishii stealth tech, they might have survived. The thought made anger flicker at the edges of Thatcher's thoughts. He'd had high hopes for the Seer scouts, and still did. It hurt to lose so many at once.

Kibishii's stealth tech has limitations. Surely Meridian's does, too. While Kibishii troop ships' stealth capabilities had seemed almost impossible when Thatcher had first encountered them, even they couldn't move around freely under full stealth. Most movement gave them away, and weapons fire certainly did.

If Meridian had vessels that remained invisible to sensors under any circumstance…

…well, such a thing could turn the tide of a war. If Daybreak's numbers didn't already do that.

A corp could likely take over the entire Cluster with ships like that. Surely they can't exist.

Either way, Thatcher had already taken the precaution of distributing drones in the space surrounding both Isovol and Isopor Stations, to act as sensor nets for allied ships—mostly as electronic countermeasures.

Maybe that will be enough to thwart Meridian's stealth.

He was about to find out.

His holoscreen's tactical display showed forty-three Daybreak ships in-system, and more were no doubt on their way.

Their fleet composition seemed to place less of a premium on eWar and logistics ships than Thatcher did, though that might have been because Daybreak had been forced to put together their fleet quickly.

Surely Frontier's successes have taught them enough about the value of support ships. Although, maybe not. Innovations in space combat didn't spread instantly throughout the Cluster, even when they led to great victories. A lot of commanders seemed stuck in the past, clinging to the tactics they'd learned from textbooks. Even Sunder's fleet was a little heavy on damage dealers, though Moll had taken most of his favorite type of ship, destroyers, with him to the asteroid belt.

What is he so keen to protect out there? So much that he'd leave his own ships vulnerable here?

Thatcher kept a close eye on his holoscreen as the Daybreak force streamed from the five jump zones to converge near the one out of Halfpace, which was closest to Isopor Station. He wondered whether the fleet commander he faced today was the same one who'd led the attack against Freedom System.

Probably not. Dirk didn't have a reputation for giving second chances, and he seemed more likely to try out some new blood for this attack.

Whoever was in charge had clearly made at least some study of the tactics that had seen play since the wormhole's collapse. He knew enough to spread his ships out as they advanced, to minimize damage against a Hellfire barrage.

But apparently no one had told him that such barrages weren't typically used by defending forces. And while the enemy formation's extreme horizontal spread protected it from that specific tactic, it left individual ships more vulnerable to getting picked off.

Almost all of Thatcher's ships had now mustered to protect Isopor. *I might as well take advantage of Sunder's love of damage dealers.* He lifted his right index finger to the holoscreen and circled a collection of ships he'd already grouped together. "*Minotaur*, take the damage dealers and support ships I'm designating and strike at this enemy logistics ship here. That will position you to take down this eWar vessel as well, once your first target goes down." He tapped the targets he meant, then made another circle, around more ships under his command. "This group will be spearheaded by *Archimedes*. Strike at this pair of logistics ships. Both groups will withdraw the instant the targets I've designated have fallen. All support ships I haven't indicated, divide yourselves among both groups. EWar, standby to execute jamming—it may be necessary to cover the retreat back to our main formation."

The command applet lit up green, and his ships sprang into action, surging toward the unsuspecting Daybreak ships. To their credit, even the Sunder captains followed his orders promptly and without question.

At first, the enemy didn't react at all, and Thatcher read surprise in the way their ships dumbly continued following their courses.

Then, as his damage dealers closed with their targets, the advancing Daybreak formation began to bunch together around the support ships that Thatcher had ordered destroyed.

But it was far too late. The logistics and eWar ships fell, and the Sunder and Frontier attackers immediately fired lasers on their secondary targets.

He pictured the Daybreak fleet commander studying his tactical display, and—once he'd figured out what Thatcher was up to—relaying his response through his Ops officer, who would contact his counterparts aboard the other Daybreak ships. Those Ops officers would then relay the orders to their captains.

It was the old way, and in comparison to Frontier's integrated comms, it was embarrassingly inefficient. Both the *Minotaur* and the *Archimedes* took some return fire from the enemy ships, but their accompanying logistics ships kept their shields healthy.

Their tasks complete, they withdrew. EWar wasn't needed to cover the retreat after all.

The enemy fleet still had two eWar vessels and three logistics ships, but Thatcher had managed to cut their support squadron in half—at least, half of what was currently represented in-system. Judging from experience, that accomplishment should have an outsized impact on the coming engagement.

Yes, Thatcher's force was still woefully outnumbered, and if Moll didn't have something spectacular up his sleeve, they were doomed. But it *would* make a difference, if only in the short term.

Something caught his eye from the tactical display, and he frowned. Eight shuttles had launched from various Daybreak ships and were now sailing toward the opposite side of the ring of jump gates, accompanied by a destroyer, two cruisers, and a corvette

They sailed directly for Isovol Station, which was completely vulnerable. Yes, Thatcher's techs had reprogrammed both refineries' turrets to target any warships that didn't match the profiles of the Frontier and Sunder ships already in-system. But the warships accompanying those shuttles would make short work of Isovol's automated defenses.

He had no idea what the shuttles' occupants intended to do once they'd boarded the station, but whatever it was, he doubted Moll would be happy about it.

He also had no way of stopping them. Right now, keeping the crews under his command alive was his top priority.

More Daybreak ships arrived in the five jump zones, including support ships to replace the ones he'd destroyed.

Damn it. He eyed the incoming enemy formation, and decided he hadn't given them enough credit for spreading out. Yes, it had allowed him to pick off their support ships, but now it prevented him from using his superior versatility to outmaneuver them. The Daybreak ships advanced in lockstep, none ranging farther ahead than the others, and they were spread perpendicular to the ecliptic as well as horizontal.

Thatcher could do nothing but retreat, now. They wouldn't let him recycle the same tactic he'd used to destroy the four support ships.

"All ships withdraw to Isopor Station. We'll adopt a circular formation around it, and hit the enemy hard, targeting ships I'll designate. If any of you think you're about to lose shields, withdraw behind Isopor. Use it as your shield. They want to retake the refinery, not destroy it."

The command applet showed him all ships had heard his orders loud and clear. The Frontier and Sunder ships reversed thrust to cluster around the refinery.

Even using Isopor as cover would only buy them so much time. Daybreak had left enough warships inside the ring of jump gates to lock down any chance of leaving Bakelite System.

Now, their only escape would be to flee toward the asteroid belt, or to break with the ecliptic and speed toward deep space. They'd be hunted like dogs either way.

The Daybreak formation drew within firing range, curling to envelop the station. Ten of their damage dealers accelerated faster than their fellows, heading straight for Isopor.

Thatcher frowned and spoke over the command channel. "Pressure those damage dealers. Don't let them neutralize the station's turret batteries."

Though the turrets were mounted on the station's hard points —reinforced portions of its hull, designed for weapon mounts— destroying them without harming the surrounding hull would prove delicate work for the enemy warships. As long as Thatcher's ships kept up the pressure, they should be able to keep the Daybreak damage dealers busy, preserving most of the station's defenses.

But the enemy ships weren't aiming for Isopor's turrets.

Instead, they loosed a stream of Hellborns aimed at the station itself.

Thatcher's mouth fell open, but he rallied quickly. "Target down those missiles!" He jabbed the panel to take himself off the fleetwide channel, then turned toward the Ops station. "Guerrero, send orders to those turrets to focus exclusively on protecting the station from the incoming Hellborns."

"Aye, sir."

Between his ships' defensive fire and that of the turrets, they managed to neutralize about a third of the missile barrage. But it wasn't enough. The rest slammed into the station's vast hull, tearing it to shreds.

The structural damage was too much, and the rest of the station succumbed to the attack, blowing wide open and flinging shrapnel in every direction.

Thatcher's breath caught in his throat. His force was now completely exposed, with Daybreak ships wrapping around them on both sides for a devastating flank.

"Retreat!" he barked over the command channel. "EWar ships, initiate omnidirectional jamming. All ships, full reverse thrust toward the asteroid belt."

The sensors went fuzzy, and the enemy fire slackened...but didn't cease altogether. Some Daybreak lasers still bit into their shields as they sped away. There were simply too many enemy ships, and their position was too good. They'd also likely anticipated Thatcher would engage omnidirectional jamming, and had already initiated electronic countermeasures.

The enemy force hadn't yet surrounded Thatcher's formation, but they hewed tightly on both sides, hammering the Frontier and Sunder ships at an increasing rate. What little effect his jamming had had was already wearing off.

The *Nautilus'* shields fell, and the ravaging lasers extended to scorch the cruiser's hull. Hellborns followed close behind, two of them impacting her starboard side near the stern. A third missile struck the same spot, blowing it wide open.

And with that, the *Nautilus* fell—a brief flash of fire and light, quickly swallowed by the void.

Next, the *Redpole*'s shields faltered, and in the seconds that followed, solid-core rounds perforated her hull. A single Hellborn was all it took to finish her off.

The enemy commander smartly targeted Thatcher's smaller ships, bagging as many kills as he could while he had such a lopsided tactical advantage. Thatcher's heart hammered in his chest as he watched a Sunder frigate go down, followed by a corvette.

Then, the Daybreak forces switched tacks, their lasers converging on the *Archimedes*. Her protective forcefield shuddered under the onslaught.

"*North Star*, bolster *Archimedes*' shields via microwave beam. All other logistics ships, deploy repair drones to her hull." It wasn't hard to tell the destroyer's shield was about to come crashing down.

The forcefield faltered just as they drew free of the harrying Daybreak ships, and a volley of enemy missiles followed up. The destroyer's point defense took down most of the attack, but several Hellborns made it through, pockmarking her hull.

The *North Star*'s rep drones lighted on the damaged areas, going to work, stitching and soldering the hull back together as quickly as they could.

With that, they were clear of the Daybreak ships—well within their firing range, but no longer surrounded.

The enemy ships sped after them, spreading even wider, to more easily thwart further jamming tactics.

We're going to lose more ships. That would be inevitable as the two forces sped toward the system's perimeter, trading blows as the Frontier-Sunder patrolling force struggled to escape.

Activity in the system's asteroid belt drew his gaze to his

holoscreen. Ships were emerging into view from behind the asteroids there. Just six at first, then eight, then three dozen all at once.

That was already more hulls than Sunder had arrived in Bakelite with. *What's going on here?*

The fleet multiplied again, their numbers expanding to seventy-three, and then eighty-five, including the original Sunder warships, which were the last to emerge into view.

Every one of the strange ships sped toward the inner system —toward the Daybreak fleet chasing Thatcher's force. The *Victorious* and her escort followed them.

"What can you tell me about those ships, Guerrero?"

The Ops officer shook her head. "I've never seen their like, Captain. They appear to be small corvettes…so small I'd almost class them as space fighters."

He frowned. "Are they automated?" The only fighters humanity had ever fielded in space were those aboard the UNC's drone carriers. Only the super-ships were large enough to house a meaningful number of them, and the drones were too small to accommodate a human pilot.

He hadn't expected an answer, but Guerrero attempted to give one anyway. "I can't tell, sir. They look big enough to house a crew of a few people, and they appear to operate independently from each other. They don't exhibit the same 'swarm' patterns that drone carrier fighters follow."

The new ships were also speedy, accelerating faster than any warship Thatcher had ever encountered, and outstripping the *Victorious'* battle group. But even accelerating under full power, it would take at least a couple hours for them to converge with the Daybreak forces.

Apparently, it didn't matter. The Daybreak fleet commander saw the writing on the wall. If he continued giving chase across the system, then soon it would be *his* force surrounded, losing ships as they scurried back toward the jump gates. The tiny corvettes were simply too fast, and too numerous.

The entire enemy force reversed thrust, then came about, accelerating toward their fellows inside Bakelite's ring of jump gates.

Thatcher tapped his armrest sharply. "We'll also reverse course. Harry them all the way to the exit, people. Give them as good as they gave us. Give them better."

Six enemy warships fell before making it to the jump gates— another eWar ship, along with a corvette, two frigates, and two cruisers. The shuttles and warships the enemy had sent to Isovol rendezvoused with the last fleeing ships on their way out.

With that, the system was quiet. Long exhales came from all over the CIC.

Thatcher switched off the fleetwide channel. "We're continuing on toward Isovol Station," he told his officers. "We'll want to know what it was they were doing over there."

A contemplative silence fell over the CIC as Bryce Sullivan and Randall Kitt worked together to bring the *Jersey* toward the refinery. What had their ally wrought, out in Bakelite's asteroid belt? What was Moll truly capable of?

And what would it cost Frontier?

They were minutes away from Isovol when the station exploded without warning. Timed charges ripped the refinery apart from evenly spaced intervals along its hull.

Both of Bakelite's refineries were gone. Thatcher hadn't expected that, and he doubted Moll had, either.

Evidently, Herwin Dirk had embraced a scorched-earth policy.

CHAPTER 30

Aboard the *New Jersey*
Bakelite System, The Splay
Earth Year 2291

MOLL HAD SEEMED IRRITATED ABOUT THE REFINERIES' destruction, but also strangely resigned, as though he'd expected it.

"If you'd deployed these new ships earlier, we might have saved them," Thatcher had said.

"Trust me, Commander. Our new fast attack ships were deployed at exactly the right time."

That statement had given Thatcher something to puzzle over for the better part of an hour. Like shuttles, the new corvettes were too small to house a reactor of any kind, and needed to be charged off another ship's reactor, or at a station. But it wasn't as though dozens of ships had suddenly become fully charged the moment before Moll had sent them barreling out of the asteroid belt. Most of them would have had full power already, and Thatcher knew each ship also carried a reserve of propellant that

Sunder chemists had created by breaking down hydrogen and oxygen from water they'd found inside Bakelite's asteroids.

So why had the man waited? The more Thatcher turned Moll's cryptic explanation over in his head, the less he understood it.

If Moll had shown his hand earlier, we likely would have destroyed fewer Daybreak ships as we chased them out of the system. The enemy would have turned tail the moment they saw all those new ships.

But the man couldn't have been so certain of that outcome that he would base such a risky decision on it. Could he?

The enemy stealth ships' location was another question plaguing Thatcher. Evidently Dirk hadn't believed he needed them to retake Bakelite. So where had he sent them?

It's possible our scout ships were bested some other way. Possible. But he couldn't think of any other way to destroy scouts in five different systems without any of them making it back to Bakelite.

Whatever the case, Thatcher needed to brief Veronica Rose on these new developments. Making decisions in light of them seemed like it was probably above his pay grade.

He gave Candle the conn and went to his office, where he used his holoscreen's connection to the *Jersey*'s instant comm unit to patch the call through.

At first he got Rose's assistant, Miriam. "I'm sorry, Commander, but Ms. Rose is in a meeting right now with shareholders. I'm afraid she'll be another twenty minutes at least. Is that okay?"

"Of course. I'll wait."

His wait ended up being much shorter than that. Miriam must have sent Rose a message about his call—within seven minutes, the holoscreen switched to a view of Rose, her pale cheeks looking faintly flushed.

Thatcher raised an eyebrow. "You cut your meeting short?"

"Of course. Nothing is more important to Frontier than what you're doing right now, Commander. Taking your calls is my number one priority. The shareholders can wait."

He nodded slowly. "Well, I'll try not to abuse that fact going forward."

"I appreciate it." A small smile formed on her lips. "I hope you're not abusing it right now."

"Moll has nanofab tech."

Her sapphire eyes widened. "How?"

"I have no idea. But I know now what he's been concealing from me, out in Bakelite's asteroid belt. He's constructed nanofabbers out there, and he's used them to construct a fleet of fast attack ships. He used that fleet to chase Daybreak out of the system, but not before they destroyed both refineries."

"That's why he brought all those mining ships and freighters with him from Candor, then. And also the real reason he wanted to take Bakelite—to use the refineries in order to secure the materials he needed, deep inside enemy territory."

"Seems so. But with the refineries destroyed, Moll's ability to continue expanding his fleet is neutered." Thatcher resisted the urge to rub his temples. Thinking about the situation they now found themselves in had given him the beginnings of a migraine. "Ms. Rose, I trust Moll less than ever. After what Boris Redding told me, and what Moll *did* to Redding..."

"I don't trust him either, Commander. But you have to see this war through, and we both know Daybreak's power can't be broken without Moll. We'll just have to deal with him once that's accomplished. We'll soon have our own nanofabbers up and running too, so we should be able to level the playing field."

Part of Thatcher wondered whether there was such a thing as leveling the playing field against someone like Moll. The man always seemed to find a way to tip it back in his favor.

But a bigger part of him reflected on his conversation with Rodrigo Aguado, on Bimaria. The meeting Thatcher had arranged, to give the UNC all the intel it could possibly want on Frontier and its activities—and its acquisition of nanofab tech.

He forced himself to inhale deeply. "With the refineries gone, the only way left for us to end the war is to take the fight out of Bakelite, to Herwin Dirk's seat of power."

Rose blinked. "Virga System? In Endysis? You want to go to Endysis?"

"It's the last thing I want to do. But if we stay here in Bakelite, we'll be starved of resources, and eventually defeated through attrition. It would also give Dirk time to launch another offensive on Oasis. Or do something we haven't thought of." Thatcher closed his eyes for a moment, then opened them to meet Rose's. "I won't let him endanger Oasis again. We have to keep him busy."

Rose swept a strand of midnight hair from her face, tucking it behind her ear. She also seemed to take a deep breath. "I…I trust your analysis, Commander."

"How are things in Freedom System?"

She sighed. "Tense. Wilson's put together a tight defense, but everyone knows we can't survive another attack on the scale of the last one. Some of the shareholders think it was insanity to send any of our ships with Moll into The Splay, let alone our best tactician. I can only imagine their reactions when I tell them I signed off on you ranging even farther afield, into Endysis."

"The shareholders don't understand war."

Rose nodded. "Which is why I retained a controlling share in Frontier. Father always said relinquishing that would be a quick path to ruin." She shook her head. "It's not just the shareholders, though. The people of New Houston are also on edge, and planetary governors from all over Dupliss have been petitioning me nonstop for more ships, and more promises that we'll come to their defense if they fall under attack. The best I can give them are conditional promises. Very conditional. We're in a tight spot here, Commander."

"I know."

Rose crossed her arms across her chest, her right hand's slender fingers gripping her left arm. "Finish this war and come home, Tad. I…feel safer with you here."

At that, they shared a long moment of silence, eyes locked on each other.

We both clearly want to say something. But neither of us is able to say it.

Almost, he told her about going to the UNC with Frontier's possession of nanofab tech.

But the last thing she needed was another complication thrown into the mix. If she lost trust in him now, while he and Moll were spearheading a mission that would determine her company's future…

He knew she was strong, but anyone might crack under that kind of pressure.

The UNC is going to do whatever it's going to. There's nothing I can do to stop it now, and there's probably nothing Rose can do, either.

The most important thing was to reopen the wormhole. To unite the Dawn Cluster, and defeat the Xanthic.

But looking into Veronica Rose's eyes, and seeing the way she was gradually letting her guard down with him, the way it had been down during the mission to Lacuna…

It killed him to consider what might be coming.

When he spoke, his voice came out a little hoarser than before. "I should go. There will be…preparations to make. Strategies to push for. And pushing anything with Moll is always a challenge."

"Good luck, Commander."

Just like that, she was back to calling him Commander.

But then, she added: "You're in my thoughts."

Almost, she added another word, but she snapped her mouth shut as it formed the first syllable.

He thought he knew what the extra word was going to be.

Always.

CHAPTER 31

Aboard the *Victorious*
Bakelite System, The Splay
Earth Year 2291

THATCHER TRAILED BEHIND BECKER, WHO SEEMED EVEN MORE reserved than usual.

Something's different about her, today. Beyond her usual standoffishness.

The *Victorious'* XO seemed…solemn. Subdued. In fact, so did every crewmember they passed on their way toward the destroyer's Strategic Planning Room—a chamber the *Jersey* lacked, due to size constraints.

Thatcher chalked the crew's mood up to the fact they'd lost both Isopor and Isovol. Preserving at least one of them had obviously been important to Moll, and it wasn't hard to see why. Losing both had come as a bit of a shock to Thatcher, but Moll had seemed only resigned. And that had evidently seeped into his crew, dragging on their morale.

In truth, he felt a little on edge himself. Not only because of their tenuous situation deep behind enemy territory, but because a large part of him smelled a trap in Moll's invitation to come aboard the destroyer and discuss strategy.

Candle had detected the same suspicious odor, and he'd wanted to come along for the visit. Thatcher had vetoed that without a moment's consideration.

He'd sniffed sharply at the suggestion. "Certainly not."

"But, sir…what if he attacks you like he attacked his own man, Redding, and then tries to cover it up?"

"That's all the more reason for you to remain aboard the *Jersey*. If it happens, then you'll be needed here, to take command of our ships and get them out of The Splay however you can."

The XO's jaw had tightened at that, and his eyes had lost their focus as he seemed to contemplate the scenario.

Escaping this region without backup would be no small feat. One Thatcher wasn't sure he'd be able to pull off himself, let alone Candle. *Hopefully it doesn't come to that.*

During the shuttle ride between the two vessels, Thatcher had thumbed idly between Attack Shuttle One's sensor feeds, and noticed the way every Frontier ship happened to drift close to the destroyer and then linger there.

Probably, they were readying themselves to turn guns on the *Victorious* if this meeting turned sour. That wouldn't be a good idea either, with Moll's vast new fleet surrounding them.

But would Moll actually try anything? According to what Redding had said in the maintenance closet, Moll saw Thatcher as a threat. Was his hubris so great that he thought he could defeat Dirk without Frontier's help?

He has to be smarter than that.

"We've arrived," Becker said. She rapped a knuckle on a panel next to a hatch, which swung open for Thatcher.

"Thanks." He entered, and the hatch closed behind him.

Moll stood at the center of the small chamber, near the controls for the holotank that dominated most of the space. He stood with his hands folded behind his back, eyes on the deck, and he didn't look up as Thatcher entered.

Like his crew, the man looked…different. His trademark sneer was replaced by a look of faint revulsion, as if he was contemplating whether a morsel he'd just swallowed had been rotten.

Thatcher took up position nearby, mimicking Moll's stance, hands clasped behind his back.

At last, the Sunder CEO spoke. "I have it on good intel that, barring something thoroughly unexpected, we're going to lose this war."

Thatcher studied the man's face carefully—what he could see of it, anyway, while it was tilted downward. In Thatcher's experience, intel was limited to things like enemy ship movements, tactics they were likely to employ, maybe leaked schematics for an upgraded weapons module.

Intelligence officers usually weren't given to projecting the success or failure of an entire campaign.

Thatcher narrowed his eyes. "If we remain in Bakelite, we'll definitely lose sooner or later."

Some of the old sneer returned as Moll's eyes snapped onto his. "Obviously we're going to leave Bakelite. But that won't make a difference."

Memories of the maintenance closet conversation with Redding returned once more. *He knows things he shouldn't,* Redding had said.

"What's the nature of this intel, exactly?" Thatcher asked.

"It's the kind of intel that isn't wrong. Ever."

"I've never encountered intel like that."

Moll closed his eyes for a long moment without answering, which only served to ratchet up Thatcher's sense of unease. What was going on here? What game was Moll playing? And how was he able to play it in the first place?

The man opened his eyes, his gaze locking onto Thatcher's

once again. "I'm handing battle tactics over to you in their entirety."

Thatcher blinked. "Come again?"

"You heard me, Thatcher. Whatever you think we should do, we'll do."

It wasn't hard to tell how difficult it was for Moll to utter those words. To admit that Thatcher's resourcefulness represented their best hope for defeating Herwin Dirk's fleets—and for returning to their homes alive.

What would cause a man like Simon Moll to concede, even to himself, that Thatcher was the better tactician?

Another man might have gloated in the face of such a concession. But Thatcher didn't feel any sense of vindication or superiority. He felt only the weight of the monumental responsibility Moll had dropped on his shoulders.

"Very well," he said. "Let's get to work."

CHAPTER 32

**Aboard the *New Jersey*
Ombrophilous System, Endysis Region
Earth Year 2291**

THE BORDER SHARED BY THE SPLAY AND ENDYSIS REGION HAD been left utterly undefended.

That, more than anything else, put Thatcher on edge. And that was saying something, as there was a lot to put him on edge during this trip to the very heart of Daybreak Combine's territory.

"We'll reach the Ombrophilous-Virga jump gate in just under a half hour, sir." Guerrero didn't turn from her console as she spoke, and her tone was measured. Almost too measured, as though she was putting it on. "Still no sign of resistance."

"Acknowledged."

Ombrophilous. Where do they come up with these names? He'd looked it up during the journey out of The Splay, and discovered it meant "tolerant of large amounts of rainfall." Out here in the farthest reaches of the Cluster, the system nomenclature got weird.

Here they were, less than thirty minutes from entering the system Paragon Industries had made its headquarters—the system from which Herwin Dirk controlled the entire Daybreak Combine—and no one was trying to stop them. Thatcher didn't like that at all.

But he had no choice.

Dirk's scorched-earth strategy hadn't been limited to the destruction of the Isovol and Isopor refineries in Bakelite. The man had likely figured out that Moll had nanofabbers, which had clearly spooked him even more than the fact of a Sunder fleet deep inside his territory.

Every station they'd stopped at had been stripped of all supplies, along with most of its personnel. Every planetary government had been warned not to lend any aid to the Frontier and Sunder invaders, with harsh retribution promised for anyone who did.

To Moll's credit, he didn't suggest forcing the civilian governments to cooperate.

Maybe that was his conscience, or maybe he knows I won't stand for it—under any circumstances. Right now, the Frontier and Sunder forces needed each other, and soon their concerns over lacking supplies would become a much less immediate issue.

Soon, they would be embroiled in the battle that would determine the fate of the Dawn Cluster.

Dirk's strategy of denying them anything useful had forced their hand. They couldn't afford to hesitate, or to run any more recon than they already had. They couldn't afford to besiege Virga system, or to wonder whether a more optimal plan existed than the one Thatcher had concocted.

Instead, they had to commit fully to the plan they had. To strike in force, while they still had the munitions to do so, and the food to feed their crews.

They had to win.

Maybe this is what Dirk wants. For us to commit fully, so he can wipe us out once and for all. Maybe he knows something we don't.

Such fears often presented themselves in the hours before an engagement. It was only natural that they'd show up before one as important as this one.

But they changed nothing.

We're in this, now. With everything we have. All the chips are on the table.

After losing all of their scout ships to Daybreak's attack on Bakelite, they'd been forced to send scouting 'squadrons' instead —a pair of warships, a logistics vessel, and an eWar ship. Thatcher had ordered the warship captains to remain ready at all times to bombard any part of empty space that showed signs of turning hostile. If that didn't work, the accompanying eWar ship could engage omnidirectional jamming.

He still had no idea what Meridian stealth ships could do now. Until he had more information about the corp's capabilities, he planned to assume that every one of their employees had transformed into some manner of space wizard.

The scout squadrons had followed parallel routes to the main force through The Splay and then through Endysis, rendezvousing frequently to report the presence of Daybreak forces following the same tack as the Frontier-Sunder force.

They also reported sighting ships that clearly belonged to pirates.

Degenerate Empire. They were sending fighting ships and freighters through the north, toward Virga System.

Apparently, the pirates had regrouped enough after the trouncing Thatcher and Wilson had administered to take their revenge by funneling warships and supplies to Daybreak. And the Frontier forces still in Dupliss, clustered around Oasis as they were, did not have enough control over the region to stop them.

Morale inside the *Jersey* ran low, and he could only imagine the situation aboard the fleet's other ships. He'd increased his personal rounds, taking walks through the cruiser's passages whenever he could spare twenty minutes, looking for those crewmembers who seemed most unsettled by the situation.

"Consider how the *Hornet*'s crew must have felt before the Battle of Midway," he said to one young petty officer who was convinced he'd never again see his parents and sister. He'd left them in Earth Local Space. "The enemy had enjoyed six solid months of unbroken success. The Japanese attack on Pearl Harbor had already devastated our battleship force, and then they went on to seize great swaths of the Pacific, to destroy the major units of the British Royal Navy, and to generally thump the Dutch, Australian, and British navies, as well as ours.

"Then they set their sights on our carriers, the *Hornet* being one of them. Imagine how frightened her crewmembers must have felt in the face of a seemingly invincible enemy. One not afraid to throw away the lives of its men to achieve its ends.

"They were right to be afraid. The battle took a large toll on them, starting with the loss of an entire squadron of bombers. Their sister ship, the *Yorktown*, was sunk. But the crew fought through their fear, and in the end, their actions proved critical to the American victory. Their warplanes ended the battle, helping to sink an enemy heavy cruiser, damaging a destroyer, and driving away the remaining heavy cruiser. The Japanese Imperial Navy never recovered, after Midway. It was a turning point in the war."

The petty officer's face was solemn after that, his jaw firm. Thatcher clapped him on the shoulder before leaving him to his duties. He told the same story to other crew who seemed to need it, as well as other stories, all about American victories snatched from the jaws of defeat. The response to Operation Drumbeat. The Battle of Yorktown. The siege of Vicksburg.

For his part, Thatcher didn't feel nearly so certain as his words suggested. He'd worked hard to formulate a plan he thought had the best chance of working, including some tactics that had never been tried before in human space combat.

It was all well and good to be inventive, but untried meant untested. The thing was, wild experimentation was their best shot at victory, and if they didn't win here today, then all was likely lost. If the Combine won, there would be no chance of uniting the Dawn Cluster—except maybe under Dirk's despotic rule.

Experimentation meant a wildly variable outcome, and that included the possibility of incredible success. Or spectacular failure. Thatcher hoped his grasp of tactics, and his ever-increasing space combat experience, would push their chances toward the success end of the spectrum.

"The jump gate has passed our checks, sir."

Thatcher blinked and looked at Guerrero, whose words had jolted him out of his thoughts. He nodded.

"We'll be ready to transition in four minutes."

"Acknowledged."

He took a steadying breath, willing his mind to focus. The problem was, there was nothing for it to focus on. The preparations had already been made, and every department knew what it had to do. Everyone was as ready as they were going to be.

And we'll be inside Virga in minutes. Focus. He turned his attention to his breathing—a mindfulness technique Lin had taught him, which normally helped him to stay present in the moment.

Today, his mind still wandered, and he realized with a jolt of shame that in the final moments of battle, he was thinking not of Lin but of Veronica Rose. Wondering what she was doing, and where *her* mind was. Whether her thoughts were with him.

His cheeks burned, and he did his best to quell his guilt, with only partial success.

Five ships transitioned ahead of the *Jersey*—all Sunder ships, other than a Frontier logistics ship.

Then, the gate seized Thatcher's light armored cruiser and flung it across the void. Seconds later, they emerged in Virga System.

A massive Daybreak fleet was arrayed around the jump zone. A Sunder cruiser's shields were about to falter. Near the *Jersey*, a frigate's forcefield was blown away, and its hull melted under a dozen enemy lasers. In less than a second, she exploded.

"Thrust hard to port," Thatcher barked at his Helm officer. "Take us clear of that shrapnel!"

CHAPTER 33

Aboard the *New Jersey*
Virga System, Endysis Region
Earth Year 2291

"COMMANDER BENJAMIN," THATCHER SAID, ADDRESSING THE commander of the logistics ship over the fleet-wide channel. "Focus on feeding the *Jersey*'s shields through our receiver array."

Without hesitation, the logistics ship turned its power-transferring microwave beam onto the *New Jersey*—as though Benjamin had been expecting the order, which he probably had been.

Without support for her shields, the Sunder cruiser whose forcefield had faltered now experienced capacitor overload and lost her protective energy barrier. The Daybreak lasers leapt past where it had been to land on her hull, melting clean through it and eating into her innards.

The cruiser exploded.

Normally, Thatcher wouldn't be prepared to unflinchingly hog logistics support for his ship alone.

But these were special circumstances.

More Sunder ships flooded the jump zone, and Thatcher directed them to the front of his formation, to absorb more enemy fire. The *Victorious* appeared as well, but it remained toward the rear, protected by the ships throwing themselves into the enemy's teeth—just as the *Jersey* was protected.

A frigate's shields shivered under the strain of seven Daybreak lasers crashing down on it. It fell, and the beams ripped the vessel apart. Another allied frigate had failed to put up any shields at all, and the enemy made short work of her.

Thatcher watched the losses stack up on his holoscreen, and he sent more ships into Herwin Dirk's meat grinder as still more appeared in the jump zone to replace them.

Lasers flashed, missiles flew, and ships came apart at the seams. Thatcher noticed a number of civilian ships fleeing the engagement, which had been unlucky enough to be near the jump zone when the fighting began. There were freighters, miners, surveyors, and transport ships—almost two dozen in total. He didn't think any of them had come to harm, which was good.

Hopefully they have the sense to stay well clear of here.

Dirk had divided his defending force between covering this jump zone and the one out of Nepheloid System—the only other ingress into Virga. Thatcher had expected as much, as well as the fact that most of the ships were concentrated on this jump gate. Dirk wouldn't be too worried about invading ships entering through Nepheloid, since to do so they would have had to go seven systems out of their way.

Moll's fast attack ships began to arrive at the engagement in quick succession, accumulating in the jump zone faster than any other class of ship could. Thatcher tapped the armrest panel that put him on the encrypted command channel and ordered these new arrivals to hang back—to avoid exposing themselves like the other ships charging toward the Daybreak fleet.

"Keep your distance, and loop around the enemy fleet on both sides. Once in position, stand by to flank."

Moll had intelligently selected his brightest personnel to crew the fast attack ships, and they executed Thatcher's orders at once, forming twin lines snaking from the jump zone even as more of the small corvettes arrived in-system.

Of course, his orders didn't come as a surprise. Not to the captains, anyway. The attack plan had already been distributed to them in encrypted data packets, programmed to self-delete after first reading. Still, Thatcher liked to reiterate everything in real time, both to bring the rest of the fleet up to speed and to remind those who'd already received the orders of their duties.

The fast attack ships sped through the void in both directions, forming the noose Thatcher aimed to choke the enemy with. But the Daybreak ships remained engaged with the ships Thatcher had flung in their face. What else could a force do when confronted with such aggression?

Those allied ships that seemed so eager to kamikaze themselves under the enemy guns were racking up a few kills, but mostly they melted under enemy lasers, or came apart under railgun fire. Daybreak was expending missiles to finish off some targets, though few were necessary. By now, they'd racked up eleven kills, in exchange for just three of their own ships.

That's right, Thatcher thought as the enemy chewed hungrily through his ships. *Enjoy your meal. I intend to make it your last.*

After Dirk's forces had been chased out of Bakelite by Moll's new fleet, Dirk would have gotten a decent estimation of how many warships the two invading corps had with them. He'd also know it wasn't possible for Moll to build many additional ships, with their destruction of the Isopor and Isovol refineries.

His estimation of the Frontier-Sunder force's size would have to be roughly equivalent to the number of their warships currently represented in this engagement.

As such, Dirk's next move made sense: to order the ships

he'd arrayed around the Nepheloid ingress to join the battle around the jump zone that led out of Ombrophilous. With almost all of Thatcher's force present and accounted for, there was no reason for Dirk to keep part of his fleet stationed at the other jump zone. When they arrived, together the two halves would crush the Frontier-Sunder invading force once and for all.

Of course, Dirk didn't have the whole story.

The man had accomplished much, but Thatcher had begun to suspect that Dirk lacked the most fundamental insight anyone could possess when it came to space warfare:

It was about deception.

The true goal of any conflict in space must be to lure your enemy into over-committing his forces, under the false assumption that he has the upper hand.

After the destruction of the twin refineries, Moll had possessed enough refined metals to construct seven more fast attack ships, and he'd been poised to do so.

Thatcher had stopped him.

Instead, he'd told Moll to program his nanofabbers to produce new designs: hollow hull sections that would be welded onto Sunder freighters, construction vessels, and mining ships.

Since everything Sunder purchased or built for itself was top-of-the-line quality, every one of these ships already had turrets for defense against piracy, and those turrets were relocated to hard points on the new hull sections. Some of the freighters even had shield modules, and the capacitors to keep their forcefields active for long enough to serve Thatcher's purpose, which would take twenty minutes at most.

The hollow hull sections altered each ship's profile such that lidar and radar would mistake them for that of a warship. In reality, they were almost toothless compared to real warships, in addition to running crewless. Instead, they were installed with simple AIs to execute transmitted course changes and to automatically target the nearest enemy ship with their modest complement of railgun turrets.

A visual check would expose the lie, but Thatcher knew most commanders rarely resorted to visual inspections of enemy ships in the heat of battle. He certainly didn't.

Eventually, one of the enemy captains would likely take a look for himself, and alert his fellows to his discovery. But by then, Thatcher expected Moll's new corvettes would be in position.

As, indeed, they now were.

He gave the order. "Fast attack ships, strike now."

The noose tightened.

Dozens of corvettes closed with the enemy fleet, sharing each target in tens. Ten lasers lighted on an enemy ship's shield, and when it went down, ten bright threads of solid-core rounds flashed from the fast attack ships' railguns.

The corvettes' small size meant they couldn't accommodate a shield module, or even missile storage. Each ship had lasers enough to knock down shields, provided they were combined with those of their sister ships, and a main railgun to finish the job.

Alone, each ship would be swatted from space by a conventional warship with ease. But swarming an enemy as they were now, they were lethal.

Target after target lost its shields and was ripped apart by the railgun rounds eating through its hull. Confusion reigned throughout the Daybreak fleet, as each captain tried to decide whether they should attack the warships that had immediately gotten in their faces or the swarming buzzards suddenly wreaking havoc on their flanks.

Hull for hull, the Frontier-Sunder fleet's kill count soon matched Daybreak's, and then surpassed it. What was more, most of the ships Thatcher had lost were dummy ships. Now, his fleet's superior positioning was exacting a devastating toll on the enemy.

But the Daybreak fleet would have been vast even if it hadn't been bolstered by reinforcements from Degenerate Empire, and Thatcher knew this tactic alone wouldn't be enough to buy him victory. The enemy captains were already regrouping, and starting the painstaking process of targeting down the fast attack ships one by one. Lacking shields, the micro-corvettes crumbled quickly.

There's no way we can take on a fleet this size with what we have in-system. Not even after outflanking them this badly.

"Guerrero, get on the instant comm. Send the signal."

"Aye, sir."

CHAPTER 34

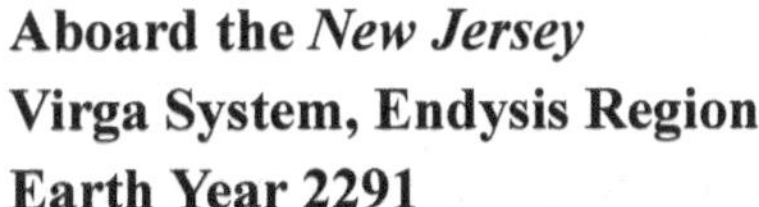

Aboard the *New Jersey*
Virga System, Endysis Region
Earth Year 2291

Guerrero sent the signal...

...and nothing happened.

More fast attack ships went down. The enemy didn't have to concentrate much firepower on any one of the micro-corvettes to rip it apart. They lacked shields, and while their hulls were solid, they had to lose something from being so hastily made.

Nanofabbers are so new.... There were almost certainly improvements and advancements yet to be made in the journey from schematic to finished ship. But to make those advancements, they'd have to survive this battle, wouldn't they?

He rapped his index finger on the panel for the command channel. For a moment, he considered limiting his broadcast to just the new ships' crews, but he decided the fleet at large would benefit from hearing their commander taking decisive action.

"Fast attack crews, I need you moving more. Take advantage of your agility and introduce some randomness into your movement. If you sit there and wait for the enemy to cut you down, then that's exactly what's going to happen."

He tapped the panel again, and within seconds the tactical display came alive with dozens of ships weaving and dodging through the battlespace. He was reminded of the guns-D maneuvers he'd learned about at the academy, during their study of historical, Earth-based battles. *With ships as small as these, that's exactly what we need to bring back.*

Part of him wanted to kick himself for failing to anticipate that, prior to this engagement. But he couldn't see everything coming. Some things, he'd just have to learn from the crucible of combat.

The evasive maneuvers slowed the rate of losses, but things would still get dire soon if nothing changed.

"Guerrero, put me through to Moll."

"Aye, sir."

There still wasn't a way for him to initiate private comms with someone aboard another ship—likely, that system would be too complicated to implement on the fly, in the heat of battle. Still…it was something to check into. Provided they survived today.

Good that I'm staying optimistic.

Moll appeared in the holotank at the front of the CIC, looming over the *Jersey* officers. He rested his bare chin on a fist, bracketed by his peculiar facial hair, which covered the rest of his jaw and connected with his mustache. "Commander. What is it?"

"We need to lead a charge through the dummy vessels. To take some of the pressure off your fast attack ships."

Moll's mouth quirked. "Losing either the *Jersey* or the *Victorious* won't do much for fleet morale. Or its prospects."

"Neither will losing half of your corvettes. If our flanking maneuver crumbles, the rest of our force will quickly follow. Our superior positioning is the only thing keeping us in this."

"Where are our reinforcements? I'd contact them myself, but I no longer have an instant comm unit." Moll placed a special emphasis on the last few words.

That was a good question. Thatcher turned toward Guerrero. "Lieutenant, what's the latest from the cavalry?"

"They say they're coming through soon, sir. Apparently they've been chasing down a Daybreak scout ship that spotted them in Nepheloid, for fear it would gain access to an instant comm unit and alert Dirk to their approach."

Thatcher's lips tightened. *They should have consulted me before embarking on that particular wild goose chase.* Risking the scout ship alerting Dirk would have been well worth it—especially considering the risk was small, given the scarcity of comm units in the Cluster, and given Dirk would know about the second force the moment they arrived in Virga anyway.

But a Sunder captain was in charge of the flanking force, which had taken a more roundabout route at full speed, one that had added seven systems to their journey to reach Virga. The plan had been to put them through the Nepheloid-Virga jump gate at exactly the right time.

The right time had been five minutes ago. Clearly, the Sunder captain in charge—Visser was his name—didn't understand the importance of letting Thatcher control every aspect of this engagement. Something Moll seemed to grasp fully.

Thatcher forced himself to take a deep breath, reminding himself that Moll's full cooperation was a rare and unexpected blessing. "Our charge will be well-supported by logistics and eWar ships, along with four damage dealers whose designations I'm transmitting to Guerrero now for forwarding to you. But we need to move now. Is that going to be a problem?" Thatcher couldn't help giving the last word an edge.

Moll's response was curt. "No. If we're doing this, let's do it." With that, he vanished from the holotank.

Thatcher put himself back on the fleetwide, spitting orders as fast as he could to the ships he wanted for the push. "Logistics, stand ready to feed power to ships that need it. EWar, I want directional jamming against any enemy vessel that targets us."

As the selected ships surged forward, Thatcher found himself marveling yet again at Moll's miraculous transformation. *What prompted him to hand over the reins to me?* Before this, the man had done everything he could to undercut Thatcher, at every turn. Now he'd done a complete one-eighty.

This plan had required a great deal of trust from Moll. He'd been extremely reluctant to disconnect his instant comm unit, which had been thoroughly integrated into the *Victorious'* systems, and hand it over to another ship. Yes, that ship also belonged to Sunder—it was Visser's destroyer, the *Damasen*—but Moll's reluctance had been palpable.

Thatcher has insisted on it all the same, and Moll had seen the sense in it. It would have been far too suspicious to send the *Victorious* with the flanking force, since the enemy would expect to see the Sunder command ship in the battlespace. It would have tipped them off to Thatcher's ruse too soon. So Moll's destroyer had handed over her instant comm, and she'd remained with the main force.

But the man's trust ran even deeper than that…so deep that it shocked Thatcher. On top of relinquishing his rare and valuable comm unit, he'd instantly agreed to sacrifice his mining vessels and freighters in order to draw fire away from the Frontier and Sunder warships.

Sure, Sunder was wealthy, and as they developed their nanofabbers and refined the schematics, they'd no doubt be able to print the parts for more such vessels.

But that still wouldn't be cheap, and it probably wouldn't happen soon. The price Moll paid today was steep. Incredibly steep.

And yet he paid it readily.

Why?

Thatcher shook himself. The battle group he'd thrown together on the fly was nearing the enemy.

Under other circumstances, he would have ordered his damage dealers to target one of the enemy's underpowered ships —one likely to have an inexperienced crew. Generally, he assumed the more losses he could rack up quickly, the lower the opposing force's morale would sink.

But Daybreak was a cat driven into a corner. A large cat. Its fleet fought fiercely to protect its seat of power, knowing that there was nowhere else to run. This single battle would decide who would rule the north…and it would decide which philosophy would prevail here, possibly throughout the entire cluster.

Daybreak would almost certainly fight to the last, and there was little Thatcher could do to change that.

So today, he was better off big game hunting.

"Lasers on the destroyer, there." He tapped his holoscreen to indicate which one, and the command applet picked it up, relaying it instantly to the other ships of his new battle group.

Bright beams sprang forward, segmenting part of the battle-space. If he was very lucky, the destroyer would belong to the fleet commander. Maybe to Herwin Dirk himself.

Is Dirk with the fleet, or safe on Cronus? Cronus was the Earth-like planet Paragon Industries had chosen for its headquarters. Remaining there would be a good way to ensure Dirk would have the chance to surrender if he lost, and to survive the day.

Except, Thatcher knew the man wasn't a coward, and like himself, Dirk was very hands-on. Chances were he'd be aboard one of the ships lingering toward the rear of the enemy formation. And a careful study of those ships would probably reveal which one.

Something to keep in mind as the battle progressed.

"Sir, our reinforcements are arriving in-system."

"Acknowledged, Guerrero." *Finally.*

That was good news, but a glance at the tactical display

tempered it: Daybreak's second force was much closer to joining the engagement. The newly arrived Frontier-Sunder force was at least ten minutes late, and those ten minutes could easily make the difference between victory and utter devastation.

The destroyer he'd marked for targeting was suffering heavy damage to its shield, and Thatcher felt good about his odds of exposing her hull to Hellborns.

Then, something changed.

He didn't need Guerrero's report to tell him what it was, but the development made him draw back from his holoscreen a few inches, and she spoke into the silence while he was still processing it.

"Sir, the Combine ships are no longer targeting our dummies. They're focusing on our battle group."

It was true. Lasers converged on the *New Jersey*, the *Victorious*, and two frigates that accompanied them. Other enemy ships were redirecting even more fire to the surrounding micro-corvettes, scoring hits by spraying solid-core rounds into the space around each target.

Space was vast, and such a volley had a small chance of connecting…but the shots fired *were* unpredictable, and with repetition the volleys were yielding results.

Thatcher was losing ships.

They've figured it out. That wasn't entirely surprising, since the second force's arrival put the Frontier-Sunder fleet at way higher numbers than they should have been able to field. Having digested that fact, it would have taken just one enemy captain to request a visual on one of the dummy ships. Moll had done everything he could to mimic a warship's hull with the hollow sections, going so far as to sculpt weapon systems that had no actual functionality.

But the devil was in the details, and even a cursory inspection of their hulls revealed them as little more than stage props.

The actual frigate nearest the *New Jersey* lost her shields, and ravening lasers bit into her hull. A two-missile follow-up finished her, flinging shrapnel in every direction, including toward the *Jersey*'s starboard hull.

Thatcher's gaze snapped onto Randall Kitt's. "Thrust hard to port."

"Aye, sir."

The *Jersey* lurched to the left, throwing the officers sideways into their restraints before the compensators kicked in. The maneuver mitigated some of the damage, but pieces of the downed frigate still rained onto his cruiser's shield, weakening it further.

Suddenly, the second enemy force's arrival felt like a death warrant. Staring hard at his target's shields, which were almost down, Thatcher made the snap call that he wasn't going to be able to take out the destroyer. Not yet, anyway.

He hammered the armrest panel with two fingers, putting himself on the fleetwide. "All ships, fall back behind the jump zone. I want every damage dealer that didn't come from a nanofabber covering our retreat."

CHAPTER 35

Aboard the *New Jersey*
Virga System, Endysis Region
Earth Year 2291

"Another ship has targeted us with its primary laser, sir. It's the frigate whose designation I'm sending your way now." Guerrero tapped smartly at her console, then made the flicking motion that would transmit the data packet. "Our shield power is down to fifty-nine percent."

"Acknowledged." Thatcher did his best to mask the grimace that threatened to contort his facial features.

The enemy fleet commander—Dirk, presumably—seemed to know that even with the two Daybreak forces united, it would be over for them if the second Frontier-Sunder fleet arrived before the first one was dealt with. If that happened, Thatcher's fleet positioning would simply be too good to withstand, and he'd make good use of the new fast attack ships to exploit the enemy's weak points even further.

And so the opposing fleet surged forward, laying on mounting pressure and seeking to break the invading force however they could. Lasers ravaged shields, bringing several dangerously low. Some allied ships already had their hulls exposed to enemy fire, and their point defense systems were working overtime to protect them from taking critical damage, paired with repair drones from logistics ships swarming over their hulls and mending what damage they could.

When Thatcher spoke again, reluctance made his words halting. "Kitt, full reverse thrust. Guerrero, tell the *Archimedes* to cover our retreat."

"Aye, sir." Guerrero began tapping out the order immediately for transmission.

He'd had no problem sending the AI-piloted dummy ships into the enemy's barrage in order to protect his own ship, which was filled with his flesh-and-blood crew. But telling the destroyer to defend the *Jersey* as she withdrew tasted a lot more sour.

Still, it would be reckless to let his cruiser's shield fall much lower. Every man and woman on this mission was counting on him to perfectly execute the plan he'd designed for them. The fact that no plan survived contact with the enemy had become a well-worn military maxim, and so on top of everything else, they needed him to innovate brilliantly. Allowing his ship to be taken or destroyed in the midst of battle would bring the opposite result.

He found himself studying Guerrero as she rapped away at her console with her usual efficiency. Some of the awkwardness that had sullied her return to the Ops console still remained, but her determination to push through it and prove that she belonged there seemed as strong as ever.

He remembered the way she'd chased him through Frontier HQ, begging him to allow her back into the CIC so she could continue carrying out her duty. An unexpected upwelling of pride arose in his chest.

She's not the woman who fell apart in Lacuna. She's grown.

He'd been skeptical that she would ever move past her break-down, and he still wasn't convinced she'd fully processed it. But for the first time, he believed she *would* get past it.

With a frown at the tactical display, Thatcher activated the command channel he'd come to rely so heavily on. "All destroyers, move to the front of the formation and cover our retreat. Logistics captains, *do not let their shields fall.*"

Almost instantly, his fleet's destroyers—mostly Sunder ships —surged forward, toward the battlefront. Microwave beams followed, connecting with receiver arrays on the big ships, as they instantly became focal points for the enemy's weapons fire. To the naked eye, the energy beams would have been invisible, but the *Jersey*'s specialized microwave radar picked them up and displayed them as yellow lines on the tactical display.

Two of the logistics ships kept themselves in 'reserve'— a concept Thatcher had discussed with them on the way from Bakelite. That pair remained near the center of the destroyer formation, ready to transfer power to a faltering shield within seconds' notice.

To make that possible, every other logistics ship had positioned itself on the outside-facing hull of the destroyer it fed power to. That left either a port or a starboard-side receiver array available for the reserve ships.

Such an arrangement had simply never been necessary before for space combat, since engagements had always occurred between a handful of ships at most. Now that the Dawn Cluster saw battling fleets with increasing frequency, these little tweaks would add up. Thatcher had almost convinced himself that the winning captain would be the one who'd figured out the most such efficiencies.

To his surprise, the *Victorious* leapt forward to join her sister ships in protecting the rest of the fleet. Predictably, she immediately drew disproportionate laserfire, and both logistics vessels kept in reserve were needed to keep her shields stable.

"Sir…." Guerrero trailed off, her hands wavering uncertainly over the Ops console.

Thatcher glanced at her sharply. "Lieutenant?"

"It's the *Archimedes*. Her shields are running dangerously low."

The holoscreen backed up Guerrero's words—the readout next to the destroyer read twenty-two percent and falling rapidly.

Thatcher winced. If the *Victorious* hadn't joined in, the logistics reserve ships might have brought those shields back into a healthier range.

I could recommend that Moll send one of the reserve ships to protect Contos' new command.

But could he ask the man to risk the *Victorious* when he'd been so careful to keep the *Jersey* safe? Provided they both survived this battle, Thatcher still didn't know whether Moll would prove friend or foe. But the man's survival could prove important to Frontier's long-term prospects.

Or it could prove ruinous.

"Send *Lancer* and *Ontario* to back up Contos."

"Aye, sir."

The cruiser and corvette captains moved to defend the destroyer just as readily as Moll had, firing lasers at her tormentors, along with a helping of Hellborns at an enemy frigate whose shield had fallen.

But the *Archimedes'* own shield now dipped into the lower teens. It seemed inevitable that her hull would soon be exposed to enemy ordnance.

We're going to lose her.

As Thatcher stared hard at his holoscreen, where the destroyer's shield readout ticked down steadily, everything seemed to slow. Suddenly, he felt like he could peer through the tactical display, through the destroyer's hull, to the crew working feverishly inside her. Each of them doing their designated task to the best of their ability, trying desperately to keep their ship intact.

Engineers, gunners, missile bay crew, CIC officers…every compartment buzzing with the shared struggle.

The thought of over a thousand lives being snuffed out all at once made him want to retch. For the moment, he'd lost the clinical distance needed to send men and women into battle to their deaths. Preventing that ship's loss became his sole purpose.

He rapped his chair's armrest panel sharply, activating the fleetwide channel. "EWar ships, prepare to coordinate an omnidirectional jamming burst on my mark. Indicate via the applet when you're ready, and stand by for my order."

His heart hammered against his chest as he watched the command applet light up green, vessel by eWar vessel. They were already spaced evenly throughout his fleet, in preparation for him giving them this very order.

For several moments, the decision to execute omnidirectional jamming felt right. It wouldn't just protect the *Archimedes*—it would also buy them time. Maybe enough time for their reinforcements to arrive, and to turn the tide of this bitter death match.

Then his eyes fell on the civilian ships—the freighters, shuttles, surveyors and transport ships—that had scurried away from the jump zone on his fleet's arrival.

For the first time, he noticed the way they were now scattered behind his ships, nearer the system's periphery than its star.

They should have fled toward Cronus. That's where they would have been safest.

Instead, the civilian vessels were spread out in scatter-plot fashion *behind* his force.

That distribution almost seemed random.

Almost.

But it wasn't. Was it?

"Belay the order to execute omnidirectional jamming," he said through gritted teeth.

There was too much intentionality to the civilian's presence, and to their formation. Because that's what it was: a formation, meant to keep sensors on every one of his ships.

They were acting as a sensor net, in effect. It had been no coincidence that those ships had been near the jump zone out of Ombrophilous in the seconds before battle was joined. Each civilian captain was almost certainly sharing sensor data with Dirk's warships in real-time.

Which meant if Thatcher had gone through with the jamming, the enemy ships would have recovered well before his own. The Daybreak fleet would have laid waste to his. No doubt Dirk knew Thatcher would never fire on civilian ships, so he'd felt assured his sensor net would be safe.

He'd been *waiting* for him to use omnidirectional jamming. Thatcher had almost handed the victory to Dirk on a silver platter.

The *Archimedes'* shield fell, and Hellborns flew from enemy missile tubes to swarm the destroyer.

It took less than a minute. Her battered port-side hull blown open, the *Archimedes* spewed flame, equipment, and crew. A handful of pressure-suited figures managed to evacuate through starboard airlocks, but Thatcher already knew most of those aboard the destroyer were lost.

The *Archimedes'* destruction freed up more enemy lasers to ravage the remaining destroyers' shields, whose power dropped faster than before. The tumbling power levels were punctuated intermittently by the destruction of more fast attack ships, which Thatcher estimated he was losing at a rate of one every minute, maybe more. He didn't have an exact count, but he didn't need one to know how desperate their situation was becoming.

The enemy was completely ignoring the dummy ships now, sailing straight past them to continue harrying the fleeing Frontier-Sunder fleet. The dummies' automatic turret fire fell on microwave-bolstered Daybreak shields, to almost no effect.

White-knuckled fingers gripping his seat's armrests,

Thatcher forced himself to look at the second Daybreak fleet. It was mere minutes away from joining the fray, and when it did, Dirk's charge would become a slaughter.

They're ignoring our dummy ships....

A flash of inspiration struck him. "Guerrero, get me Ensign Devine."

The lieutenant shot him a confused look, but to her credit, she didn't hesitate. The young engineer was soon in his ear.

"Captain?" he asked, sounding just as bewildered as Guerrero had looked.

"Ensign." Technically, Thatcher should have contacted Marat, who'd been promoted to Commander and chief engineer after Ainsley had died during the battle in Ucalegon. But while Marat was competent, he didn't have Devine's quickness. "How quickly can you reprogram the AIs aboard those construction and mining ships?"

"R-reprogram them, Captain? We installed them manually, directly into the consoles."

"I asked a simple question, Ensign. I need a simple answer."

"I—well, I guess I should be able to gain root access remotely, come to think of it. I'm not sure what changes you want, sir, but anything complicated is going to take a while, especially since we're talking about dozens of ships that'll need reprogramming...."

Devine trailed off, and Thatcher allowed their conversation to lapse into silence. It wasn't hard to tell the ensign's mind was turning over rapidly, like a finely tuned engine.

"Come to think of it, I should be able to whip up a macro for working on them all simultaneously. The macro itself will take time, but it'll be a lot quicker than reprogramming each AI individually. And actually, I can adapt it from one I've been using to calibrate the sensors that monitor the reactor's stochastic power fluctuations."

"Don't tell me about it, Devine. Do it. Every second is precious."

When Devine spoke again, he sounded breathless with excitement. "Yes, sir." With that, he was gone.

Thatcher returned his attention to the battlespace, where the pursuing Daybreak ships were reaching past the line of destroyers with their weapons, claiming a Sunder frigate, followed almost immediately by two attack ships.

Hundreds more souls lost to the void. Lost to history.

Hundreds more families who'd mourn.

The only consolation, if one could call it that, was that many of those families were likely still in Earth Local Space, and wouldn't learn of their loved ones' deaths for a long time yet. Instead, they would live in hopes of their return.

In hopes that the wormhole would reopen, someday.

That was assuming the Xanthic hadn't already burned down Earth Local Space, and slaughtered everyone in it.

Thatcher's eyes ached as he scanned the tactical display, searching desperately for opportunities.

I need to do better.

CHAPTER 36

Aboard the *New Jersey*
Virga System, Endysis Region
Earth Year 2291

ANOTHER SUNDER DESTROYER, THE *GERYON*, LOST HER SHIELDS and began to come apart at the seams under enemy fire.

Hellborns rained down on her, blowing apart entire sections of her hull, and Thatcher didn't have the stomach to call up a close-in visual.

He knew the sight that would greet him if he did. The things he'd watch ejected, helpless, into space.

The lost souls. With no pressure suits, no hope of getting picked up by a friendly ship in time, even if they survived the deadly shrapnel their vessel was flinging in multiple directions.

Geryon had occupied a central point in the destroyer formation fighting desperately to hold the line and defend their allied ships. She'd taken up a position near the *Victorious*, and Moll's ship was forced to move away to avoid the shrapnel.

Daybreak smelled blood in the water, and still more ships targeted the wounded destroyer.

The damage crossed a critical threshold, and the beleaguered warship lost her structural integrity. She disintegrated, a quickly-smothered conflagration her only legacy.

Still nothing from Devine. Thatcher felt a sharp pain in both palms, and realized he was clenching his fists so tightly that even his well-trimmed nails bit into the flesh there. Blinking down at them, he forced his fingers to uncurl.

Candle was looking at him, concern etched across his features. Thatcher shook his head curtly, and the XO returned his gaze to his own console.

"Sir."

He turned to face the Ops station, his heart sinking even further. That hoarse syllable had held as much tension and worry as Thatcher had ever heard from Guerrero. She sounded worse than she had before her breakdown in Lacuna.

When she spoke again she sounded a little better, though not much. "Sir, the other enemy fleet is here."

He wanted to squeeze his eyes shut and massage his temples. Instead, he forced himself to confront the reality his holoscreen depicted.

His grandfather's voice came to him, then. And though he hadn't closed his eyes, images flooded his mind all the same.

"Take your hands from your pockets, Tad."

Tad had snatched them out before Edward Thatcher had finished his sentence, already knowing what his grandfather was going to say. He'd said it a million times before, calling it a bad habit.

"Why?" Tad asked—something he'd never thought to ask before.

He'd expected a rebuke, but instead the question brought a smile to his grandfather's face. Edward had nodded. "That's a good question. Why. Helps to understand the principles behind things. And if you can grasp those, you can start using them to your advantage. I'm glad you asked."

Tad continued walking, frowning slightly, and resisting the urge to stick his hands back into his pockets. His grandfather still hadn't answered the question, so he waited patiently. Patience was another virtue, according to Edward Thatcher.

"People with their hands in their pockets have something to hide. Maybe it's a knife, or maybe just an ugly thought. There will be times you'll need to hide something, but you'd better have a better place to hide it than your pockets. And you'd better keep your hands well away from wherever you've hidden it. You need to be more clever than the people who walk around with their hands in their pockets all the time. More subtle."

Tad decided that was a very good answer, and he silently vowed never to put his hands in his pockets again.

"Listen to that, Tad." His grandfather's gaze wandered over the Heartland of America Park, across the Missouri River, to where a gang of children played some chaotic game of their own invention. Their delighted squeals and shouts drifted across the water to reach the concrete boulevard along which Tad and his grandfather walked. "If you're going to fly with Space Fleet, then that's what you'll be protecting. Listen to that sound. That's the essence of it, there."

The sound of children's laughter faded away, leaving Thatcher staring at his holoscreen. Less than a second had passed, but somehow, he'd found the strength to be fully present in this moment.

A profound sadness underlaid his new sense of calm confidence. He still missed Edward Thatcher dearly.

He tapped the panel to put himself on the fleetwide. "We need to prevent that second fleet from getting a flank on us." His finger dragged a rough outline across the tactical display, designating thirty-four fast attack ships. "The micro-corvettes I've indicated will move to confront the enemy, keeping your movements as unpredictable as possible. Take down as many shields as you can. Spook them. I want every eWar vessel to accompany our fast attack ships, and jam the targeting of any enemy ship that tries to take down one of our micro-corvettes."

The ships he'd designated leapt into action, even as more allied ships fell.

Damn it, Devine. Where are you?

Anxiety reared its head again, threatening to annihilate his newfound calm. If he didn't hear from the young engineer soon, there was simply no way they'd pull through this.

Even so, he didn't dare contact Devine, for fear of distracting him at a critical moment.

Sometimes, the best thing a captain could do was trust his crew.

He found himself wondering what Moll was thinking, right now. The man had been certain this battle would end in defeat—so certain that he'd handed over total control to Thatcher.

It was beginning to look like that wouldn't make a difference, either.

What made Moll do what he did? What caused his change of heart toward me?

Would Thatcher live to find out?

His comm beeped, and he plucked it from its resting place atop his console. "Thatcher here."

"Sir, it's me. Devine. I'm ready to have those ships do whatever you'd like them to."

"Excellent. I want you to remove the subroutine that has them auto-firing on the nearest enemy and get ready to have them concentrate their fire on a target whose designation I'll send you."

"Can do, sir. Just let me know when you're ready."

Thatcher tapped the armrest panel without wasting the time it would take to answer. "All ships along the battlefront, prepare to divide laserfire between the targets I'm designating now." He tapped the icons representing an enemy destroyer and a cruiser of a similar make to that of the *New Jersey*. "I've sent the designations. Fire on my order. As soon as the targets' shields fall, I want you to immediately switch to other targets whose designations I will transmit momentarily. Acknowledge receipt of orders."

Ship by ship, the command applet lit up green—filling up with the color faster than he'd yet seen.

"Fire lasers."

Blue beams shot across the battlespace, creating a lopsided spider's web that converged on two enemy vessels.

Thatcher switched back to the private channel with his engineer. "Devine. All ready?"

"Ready, Captain."

"Sending you the target's coordinates."

The enemy destroyer's shield fell within seconds of forwarding the data.

"Have our AIs fire on it now."

After learning to ignore them, the enemy fleet had bypassed the freighters and mining ships, treating them like harmless gnats which they allowed to occupy positions distributed throughout their formation.

Now, those gnats turned into a deadly, unified swarm. Their turrets fired in tandem on the destroyer's exposed hull, and she burst apart within seconds.

"Now this cruiser." Thatcher sent the designation.

Target after target went down in quick succession, his warships taking down their shields for the empty miners and freighters to finish the job.

Thatcher chose only targets which his AI-piloted vessels already had surrounded. Dirk had unwittingly allowed a deadly weapon to be inserted amongst his ranks.

Clearly spooked by the rapid losses, the first enemy fleet recoiled, trying to pull back beyond the empty vessels.

Not on my watch. "All ships, reverse course. Give chase and let them have it."

The Frontier-Sunder force surged forward, and Thatcher continued designating targets. His warships blew away their shields, and Devine's massive drones finished them off.

The second Daybreak fleet wasn't compromised by dozens of enemies in its midst, and it redoubled its efforts to fight through and help out their first fleet. But the eWar ships' targeted jamming was proving effective, and Thatcher's fast attack ships struck in swarms, taking apart one blinded ship, then another.

Beyond the second enemy fleet, Thatcher's reinforcements spread themselves wide, preparing to brutally outflank the enemy.

And outflank them they did. The force that had traveled deeper into Endysis, adding seven systems to their journey, now reaped the fruits of the extra effort.

The Daybreak force was almost completely surrounded, and here, Thatcher's integrated comms truly shone. While the enemy fleet commander struggled desperately to answer Frontier-Sunder's renewed assault, firing on their ships haphazardly, Thatcher was able to efficiently allocate his firepower, devoting just enough to take down each target before moving on to the next.

His force ground away at the enemy like an inexorable machine, until Guerrero turned to announce a transmission request from one of the enemy destroyers.

Thatcher gave the nod, and Herwin Dirk appeared in the holoscreen at the front of the CIC. Twin strands of black hair had escaped the man's mop to dangle over his bearded face. He seemed to notice them, sweeping the stray hairs away from his face with a grimace.

Thatcher restrained the urge to mirror Dirk's grimace—mostly due to the Daybreak leader's unkempt appearance. *A man who looks like that should never be allowed at the helm of a warship, let alone a super-alliance.*

He'd seen photos of Dirk before, of course, but somehow the

man's present desperation underscored his lack of professionalism.

"Thatcher, isn't it?" Dirk rasped.

"It is."

"Surrender. I offer you my surrender. Stop attacking my ships. Paragon Industries will withdraw from this conflict, along with all the corps under my command. We'll resume our normal activities."

A terse chuckle escaped Thatcher's lips. "Somehow, I doubt it will be quite that simple." He narrowed his eyes. Would Dirk have shown him any mercy, had their positions been reversed?

Of course he wouldn't. But that was what separated them— not only as starship captains, but as men.

"I'm prepared to accept your surrender." He cleared his throat, then added, "Your *unconditional* surrender."

Dirk winced, and for a moment it seemed he would argue. Then he spoke again. "You have it."

Thatcher exhaled in a rush of air. "End the transmission, Guerrero."

The leader of the now-defunct Daybreak Combine vanished from the holotank. On the tactical display, the enemy weapons fire dried up.

Thatcher tapped the armrest panel one more time.

"All ships, cease firing. I repeat. Cease firing."

CHAPTER 37

Aboard the *New Jersey*
Virga System, Endysis Region
Earth Year 2291

THATCHER REMEMBERED LIVING UNDER A DEMOCRATICALLY elected government, rather than a star cluster with a hodgepodge of civilian colonies serviced by countless warring corps.

During election seasons, the ugliest skeletons had always been dragged from political closets. Damning secrets whose reveals were far too conveniently timed to be mere coincidence.

In a very similar fashion, the revelation that Daybreak Combine's leadership had been fully aware of Meridian's stealth attacks against Kibishii—and had done nothing to stop those attacks—came at the perfect time. It served as the final nail in the super-alliance's coffin, and corps were fleeing it in droves, self-conscious of the stink that clung to them and doing anything they could to placate an enraged public. Driven by widespread threats of boycott, they did whatever they could to distance themselves from anything Herwin Dirk had ever touched.

Even Dirk's own corp, Paragon Industries, pulled out of the

Combine. That was amusing. The company's stock had already crashed through the floor, and every indication was that Paragon was doomed.

"The leak was Mittelman's work," Veronica Rose said from a holoscreen, her tone one of satisfaction mixed with pride. "One of his spies broke into Dirk's email last week, and now seemed like the perfect time to use what he found."

Thatcher cocked an eyebrow and glanced around the chamber, to gauge the reaction from the Frontier captains sitting around the conference table. A few of them shifted in their seats, seeming to contemplate the information.

It didn't take a mind reader to discern what they were thinking: *Why didn't Rose have the information leaked last week, when it might have made a difference to the engagement?*

Maybe it wouldn't have done anything to change the battle. The corps of the Daybreak Combine were fighting to defend a region where many of them were headquartered, after all. Indeed, many of them were based in this very system. And who knew what other means Dirk might have had for keeping them under his control, before Thatcher and Moll had deposed him? Probably he'd controlled much of their resources, and many of their assets.

Maybe it wouldn't have made a difference.

Maybe.

Either way, the leak was certainly doing damage now. The Combine's disintegration was complete.

I'm sure Rose knows what she's doing. Besides, questioning her had brought Thatcher nothing but trouble, and it would bring him more yet—when she discovered what he'd shared with the UNC.

That didn't mean he'd stop questioning when he believed it was necessary, of course.

Call it a fatal flaw. "Have the stealth ships been secured?"

Rose nodded, her exuberance dimming a little. "Yes, thank

God. We don't have to worry about them anymore. And we can finally figure out how Meridian managed to get close enough to our scouts to destroy all of them without being detected."

Thatcher had expected the stealth ships to hit his fleet during the battle for Virga System, but apparently Dirk had been so confident in his prospects for victory that he'd sent them to attack Freedom System instead.

Dirk had called off that attack after losing, and relinquishing the stealth ships to Frontier had been a condition of his surrender. But a shiver ran along Thatcher's spine as he contemplated what might have happened if the stealth ships had reached Oasis. The fact they hadn't reached the colony constituted the sort of good luck that made him profoundly uncomfortable. He hated being beholden to luck.

Even so, he relished the thought that with the secret of stealth tech, he could realize his vision for Frontier's Seer-class scout ships. The intel the new tech would allow them to gather would prove an incredible force multiplier. He felt sure of that.

Loretta Duncombe, captain of the *Minotaur*, crossed her arms. "Are you letting Sunder have access to the new stealth tech?"

Rose had insisted on including several of the captains under Thatcher's command in this meeting, because she'd wanted to get the best picture possible of what was happening in Endysis. She knew that meant talking to people on the front lines—people who actually knew what was going on.

It was a rare quality in leaders, to consult with subordinates and use their input to inform decisions. Of course, these captains were all long-time Frontier employees. People Rose knew she could trust. But she also knew they weren't afraid of speaking their minds, and Thatcher respected that she included them anyway, despite knowing she might face criticism from them.

Captain Wilson, who occupied a holoscreen to the right of Rose's, spoke up to answer Duncombe's question. "We all know

Moll expects access to the stealth tech. Frankly, we don't know how our relationship with Sunder will look going forward. Right now, we need them, so we're doing our best to stall handing over the tech."

Rose nodded. "Eventually, it will come to a head. We'll need to either give Moll the tech or declare Sunder Incorporated our enemy. Neither are attractive options." She shrugged, slim shoulders rising to send some of her raven hair cascading down her upper arms. "The decision may soon be made for us. The rest of the Cluster has already begun to show signs of turning against Moll. Word of Captain Boris Redding's death has spread, and it isn't seeing a very positive reception."

Duncombe shook her head sharply, arms still crossed. "Most of the Cluster's corps are cowering dogs looking for a strong master. They're likely to fear Moll as much as they hate him. A dog will obey a master it fears, even if it hates him."

"There is some good news," Hans Mittelman cut in. The holoscreen on Rose's left showed his rodent-like face in three dimensions. "A new alliance has risen from the chaos of the south. An industry-focused alliance, with values that seem to align more or less with Frontier's. Their goals suggest such an alignment, at any rate: peace, stability, and prosperity for their corporate members and the colonies under their protection. Their name is somewhat fitting, too: Ascendant Horizon."

"Ascendant Horizon's emergence might be just in time," Rose added. "Sunder clearly has nanofabbers in the south as well —a new fast attack fleet just conquered most of Lament Region. Moll wouldn't use the word "conquer," of course. He'd say that he's bringing stability to the region. But we'll call it what it is. Annexation."

Thatcher cleared his throat. "What should our fleet's position be toward Sunder?"

Rose's lips tightened. "For now, we have to work with Sunder. Daybreak's collapse has left an enormous power vacuum, and the aftermath could become worse than the war, if we let it. We don't want Daybreak to somehow reemerge, and we certainly don't want a situation like the one the south is only now pulling itself out of." The Frontier CEO met each captain's eyes in turn. "But be careful. Moll clearly has an agenda, and the chances seem high that he'll try to implement some new policy that Frontier simply won't be able to tolerate. I fear that would bring things to a head much sooner than I hoped."

The meeting wound down after that, with Rose commending her captains on their recent performance in battle.

Thatcher could tell she was trying to keep things as upbeat as she could. For that reason, he chose not to bring up the threat Rose had neglected to mention at all during this meeting: Degenerate Empire.

They still held five regions, and judging from the ships and supplies they'd been able to send Daybreak, the pirates were rallying quickly from the beating Thatcher and Wilson had laid on them. Worse, reports had reached him of more pirate vessels streaming north to join the Empire as the south stabilized.

Frontier would need to deal with them quickly, to have a shot at defending the north from the next Xanthic attack.

But that wasn't all. Since the battle with Daybreak had ended, one thing had been tugging at Thatcher's thoughts, like an itch he couldn't scratch.

He couldn't stop thinking about Nankeen System, in Lacuna region. And how single-minded the pirates had been about keeping everyone else out.

What would give a bunch of disorganized pirates that level of resolve?

A large part of him wanted to know the answer.

A larger part feared it.

EPILOGUE

Aboard the *Victorious*
Virga System, Endysis Region
Earth Year 2291

As he listened to the end of the Frontier meeting, Moll sat ramrod straight in his office chair, staring into space, expressionless.

Thatcher's voice came through the bug planted in the *New Jersey*'s conference room with only a little distortion. "What should our fleet's position be toward Sunder?"

Veronica Rose answered. "For now, we have to work with Sunder. Daybreak's collapse has left an enormous power vacuum, and the aftermath could become worse than the war, if we let it. We don't want Daybreak to somehow reemerge, and we certainly don't want a situation like the one the south is only now pulling itself out of."

There was a pause, then Rose continued. "But be careful. Moll clearly has an agenda, and the chances seem high that he'll try to implement some new policy that Frontier simply won't be able to tolerate. I fear that would bring things to a head much sooner than I hoped."

After that, the Frontier CEO imparted a few hollow words of encouragement to her captains, and the meeting ended.

Moll sat in the silence that followed for a long time, marinating in it.

I should feel something, after defeating Dirk. A sense of accomplishment. Excitement for what's to come. Anything.

He felt nothing. Or at least, barely anything. His emotions were all shades of gray, now.

Except for one.

Hatred.

Something happened when you took a life's natural progression and threw it out of joint, he'd learned. Events lost their color. Their meaning.

People became meaningless, too. Their lives. And their souls, if indeed they had them.

People he'd killed, again and again…enemies, colleagues, friends. Everyone was disposable to him, now. Mere means to a single end.

Moll stood, his chair gliding backward to *thump* against the bulkhead. He crossed the office to his strongbox and punched in the code to open it.

The door hissed open horizontally. Inside were two shelves, and nestled against the back of the top shelf was a framed photograph. He gently removed it, holding it in both hands and staring down at the eighteen-year-old girl it showed.

Blond ringlets framed a perfect face. There had been a time when the very sight of her would bring tears to his eyes. More than once, his tears had splashed onto the glass protecting the image.

No more.

Did he even love her anymore?

Did he truly want her back, or did he only want to kill the

man who'd taken her from him—the man who'd kidnapped her, defiled her, then killed her?

I need to make this work. This time, it has *to work.*

He knew he wouldn't last many more cycles. His body couldn't take it.

Thatcher had seen him through the Battle of Virga—an engagement that had thwarted Moll many times before.

He'd managed to win it just once, many cycles ago, only to later be thwarted by another massive roadblock. It had taken him too long to find the humility to admit to himself that he would need help in order to win Virga again.

Thatcher's help.

But would Thatcher get him past the final challenge, which Moll knew still lay ahead?

He stroked the pale, oval face in the photo with the second knuckle of his index finger.

He spoke to it.

"I will make this cluster burn for you, Elise."

GLOSSARY OF DAWN CLUSTER
CORPORATIONS

Celeste Security Solutions

CEO: Selene Williams

The emergence of Celeste Security Solutions represents a number of innovations, for space warfare generally and Dawn Cluster geopolitics specifically.

Celeste's CEO, Selene Williams, formerly worked as an engineer for Neptune Gases, a startup seeking to disrupt the atmospheric mining industry through its proprietary tropospheric aerostats—buoyant stations designed to weather the harsh conditions of gas giant tropospheres in order to harvest the denser, more valuable gases found there.

Following the wormhole's collapse, shareholder anxiety over mounting instability prompted Neptune Gases to relocate its operations from Dupliss Region's Mislit System to Paciferous System in Unity, where they would enjoy the heightened security of operating in a cold region, under the protection of UNC superships.

In Williams' own words, "Where the shareholders found reasons to be afraid, I saw opportunity."

She quit her job with Neptune and immediately began seeking funding for a new type of corp: one that would specialize in providing consulting and military services to corps interested in bolstering system defense, primarily in order to secure their headquarters.

Most investors Williams approached turned her down, unwilling to tolerate the risk that the UNC would continue to enforce its prohibition of corp-on-corp warfare throughout the Cluster. Many investors also cited Williams' lack of experience commanding military operations, unimpressed by her eight years with the British Royal Space Fleet, which included five years as a senior rate.

However, Williams soon attracted an enthusiastic funder in trillionaire August Ducas, a man with a reputation for investing in socially unpalatable businesses that go on to quickly generate enormous dividends.

At the time of writing, Celeste has found its first client. In a move that shocked analysts, Frontier Security, a corp that has staked its own reputation on upholding the public good, hired Celeste to defend Freedom System against the attacking Daybreak Combine. While the move was almost certainly borne of desperation, Frontier was perhaps the last company anyone would have expected to hire what was essentially a mercenary corp. The contract between Frontier and Celeste sent a signal to interstellar markets that a new trend was developing, and Celeste's stock rose faster than that of any other space-faring corp in modern history.

Celeste's successful defense of Freedom System drew heavily on Selene Williams' knowledge of gas giant tropospheres, and the requirements for operating there. However, in an interview given since the engagement, Williams insisted that "Celeste is not a one-trick pony. We're already developing new methodologies and technologies in order to give each new client the edge they will need to protect operations from aggressors."

Whether Celeste's emergence truly represents a developing trend in Dawn Cluster space warfare remains to be seen.

Frontier Security

CEO: Veronica Rose

CIO: Hans Mittelman

Frontier is a security firm that prides itself on upholding American values. Founded in Earth Year 2259 by Rear Admiral Gregory Rose, his daughter Veronica now runs the company. Her stated intention is to stay true to her father's vision.

Currently, Frontier forms part of the Oasis Protectorate, a conglomerate formed for the purpose of servicing and protecting American colonies located throughout the Dawn Cluster's Dupliss Region.

Kibishii

CEO: Akio Hata

COO: Theodore Xu

Kibishii is a Japanese PMC (private military company), incorporated in Earth Year 2279. The company specializes in stealth troop mobilization as well as stealth detection technologies, and in EY 2288 it opened an asteroid mining division, the expansion of which is now one of Kibishii's primary focuses.

Meridian

CEO: Oliver Breckinridge

CIO: Ezra Yates

Headquartered on Valkyrie Station, in the Herward System, Kreng Region, Meridian has positioned itself as the only Dawn Cluster corporation with such a narrow focus on stealth technology, which it both implements on its own warships and sells to client PMCs and governments. Its main competitor in the north is the Japanese company Kibishii.

Analysts suggest that Kibishii's pursuit of stealth detection technology has recently spurred Meridian to innovate wildly, with expectations high for whatever its next product offering will be.

Paragon Industries

CEO: Herwin Dirk

Paragon Industries began in Earth Year 2262 as an asteroid mining company with a specialty in exploiting planetesimals. However, after repeated attacks disrupted their operations, they acquired a small fleet of warships for protection. The attacks that prompted this move were ostensibly perpetrated by pirates, though CEO Herwin Dirk has gone on the record with claims that the true culprit was a Russian PMC operating in the area at that time.

As it gained years of experience defending mining operations, Paragon Industries gradually transformed into a highly successful, multi-stellar PMC that now mainly offers security services to mining company clients.

Reardon Interstellar

CEO: Ramon Pegg

Founded in Earth Year 2210, Reardon was one of the first PMCs to offer its services in the Dawn Cluster, in response to a growing threat from pirates based in the Contested Regions. Reardon identifies as an American company, but has also accepted contracts from various US trading partners, along with countries that have less-certain relationships with the USA, including China and Russia. In response to media inquiries concerning these latter contracts, Reardon CEOs have typically pointed out that, with the rise of the United Nations and Colonies, war between nations has become virtually extinct. It is therefore foolish to turn down any contracts.

Reardon has consistently denied rumors alleging the company has engaged in hot-system skirmishes against other Dawn Cluster corporations. Reardon forms part of the Oasis Protectorate, however at the time of writing its position within the Protectorate has been called into question, with allegations being forwarded by multiple interested parties that the company has been consorting with pirates.

Red Sky

CEO: Mikhail Volkov

Red Sky is a Russian PMC headquartered in Gabbro System, in The Brush. However, at the time of writing Red Sky has vacated The Brush entirely following a dispute with Sunder Incorporated. The details surrounding this dispute are muddied by the fact that both corps give directly contradictory accounts of the events leading up to it.

Red Sky's marketing specifically targets Russian clients, however CEO Mikhail Volkov has claimed on multiple occasions that Western corps simply won't do business with Red Sky, for no reason other than that Red Sky is a Russian corp.

Sunder Incorporated

CEO: Simon Moll

Sunder holds the distinction of being the first PMC to accept a security contract within the Dawn Cluster. While headquartered in Candor, a Cluster Region, the company draws its employees mostly from European countries and colonies, primarily German and Swedish. Sunder was founded in 2208 by a former UNC dreadnought commander, Captain Patrick Moen, and the company has only had two CEOs since its inception—Moen and Simon Moll.

In the 2250s, Spanish biographer Luis Borges made the claim that Moen and Moll were the same person. As evidence, Borges highlighted Moll's lack of a documented past before his involvement with the company, the fact there is nothing to indicate the Sunder CEOs have ever met, and a number of physical similarities between the two men. Borges claimed that Moll underwent extensive cosmetic surgery to change his identity, though he did not advance any theory of why Moll would go to these efforts.

In recent decades, Borges' claims have been dismissed as fringe conspiracy theory, since in order for them to be true, Moll would have to be in excess of 160 years old—twenty-seven years older than the eldest human being ever documented.

A NOTE ON DAWN CLUSTER CARTOGRAPHY

In the Dawn Cluster, cardinal directions are used for ease of reference, with the black hole at the galaxy's center acting as a "north star."

Terms such as north, south, east, and west are meaningful because of the Cluster's layout. While star systems *are* distributed along the Z-axis, with a maximum spread of 13.781 light years, the Cluster's X- and Y-axes are much longer, at 105.134 light years and 81.240 light years respectively.

ACKNOWLEDGMENTS

Thank you to my Alpha Team, who have been reading this book since its earliest stage and who've provided substantial feedback along the way, which helped me develop the story with my readers' desires foremost in mind. They are Rex Bain, Sheila Beitler, Bruce Brandt, Colin Oliver, Jeff Rudolph, Ben Varela, and Leo Vaccaro.

Thank you to my proofreading team, who helped eliminate scores of spelling and grammar issues. I take full responsibility for any mistakes that remain :) My proofreaders are Rex Bain, Sheila Beitler, Bruce Brandt, and Jeff Rudolph.

A special thank you to my Patreon supporters at the Space Fleet Admiral level. Your support helps me to package my books as professionally as possible while staying true to what my readers like best about my books. My Space Fleet Admiral patrons are Eldon Adams, Brian Loeung, David Middleton, and Michael Van De Hey. Thank you so much.

Thank you also to Patreon supporters Lucian Ban, Richard Gunn, Alex Hamilton, Christian Kallias, John A Koenig III, Luke Lofgren, Daniel Mabry, Owen Messerly, Jason Pennock, Wynand Pretorius, John Tava, Ben Varela, and Jerry Winiarski.

Thank you to Jason Carayanniotis and Chris Evans for helping me flesh out the details for how some of the technology in the book works.

Thank you to Tom Edwards for creating such stunning cover art, as always.

Thank you to Steve Beaulieu for creating striking typography and for formatting this print book.

Thank you to my family - Mom, Dad, and Danielle - your support means everything.

Thank you to the people who read my stories. I couldn't do this without you.